101 THINGS EVERY YOUNG ATHLETE SHOULD KNOW

Master Goal Setting, Mental Toughness, Perseverance, Teamwork, Discipline, Nutrition, Injury Prevention, and More!

Taylor Marr

FREE BONUS

SCAN TO GET OUR NEXT
BOOK FOR FREE!

Table of Contents

INTRODUCTION

When you think of the word *athlete*, you might envision a professional baseball or soccer player, an Olympic gymnast or skier, or even someone you know who is great at sports all around. But just as there are numerous types of athletic competitions, there are also many kinds of athletes.

An athlete is generally considered to be a person who is skilled in a particular sport or physical exercise and often puts their skills to the test in competitive games or events. This can include everything from track and field events to swimming to archery — and all the other sports out there. Whether you're a beginner or an experienced athlete, there are some common things that you should know to ensure that your athletic journey is safe, meaningful, and fun.

This book is designed for athletes of all ages who are involved in any sport. The goal is to provide basic topics and information that will benefit you as you begin your sports journey. This includes advice regarding good sportsmanship; proper warm-up and cool-down routines; eating nutritious foods and staying hydrated; adapting to change; and avoiding conditions such as overtraining, injury, and burnout. These strategies will not only improve your athletic performance and overall experience, but they will also provide you with encouragement to take care of your physical and mental health now and in the future.

Learning to play a sport is a valuable experience that offers short and long-term rewards such as building physical health, emotional strength, social skills, and self-confidence. Yet it's often much more complex than just understanding the rules of how to play or practicing certain physical skills related to the sport. Even at a young age, athletes must navigate relationships with teammates, opponents, coaches, and more.

In addition, participating in a sport requires time commitment, mental focus, and the ability to balance other life activities.

Athletes must also learn to handle victories with humility and cope with losses in a resilient manner. That's why it's important to learn as much as possible from guides such as this one; you'll learn to be prepared for the range of emotions, challenges, and meaningful experiences that are sure to accompany you on your athletic journey.

This guide can be read from front to back, or you can scan the topics to find which are most relevant to you. Each subject is presented in a way that allows you to refer to it as often as needed; you can also share the information, strategies, and ideas with your teammates, coaches, parents, and friends.

Of course, there are things that young athletes should know that go beyond the 101 ideas presented here. It would be almost impossible to list or address everything that you might encounter as a player. However, the information and strategies included in this book are meant to establish a practical foundation of support, learning, and confidence. This will allow you to maximize the life experience, personal strength, and fun memories that come with being an athlete.

And so, without further ado, let's dive into 101 Things Every Young Athlete Should Know!

[1]
SET GOALS

Apart from being an important life skill, knowing how to set goals is a large part of having a successful athletic journey. As you achieve each personal objective you plan, you'll find the goal-setting process rewarding and be able to apply those strategies to other areas of your life. Just like playing a sport, setting goals requires focus, commitment, and practice.

A short-term goal is something specific you want to achieve in the near future that involves quick, straightforward steps to achieve. In sports, a short-term goal might be to improve the time it takes for you to run a mile or increase the number of reps in your weight-lifting routine. Long-term goals tend to be more general objectives for further on down the line. They can be adapted over time and are often made up of smaller, short-term goals.

As a young athlete, you may set a long-term goal of playing a sport at the varsity level in high school or competing at a regional or state level once you reach a certain age division. Setting goals for both the near and distant future helps you focus on what you'd like to achieve and create a path toward success. In the short term, celebrating the completion of smaller goals can help you stay motivated to reach your larger, more involved objectives.

If you aren't sure how to set goals for your athletic journey, take some time to consider what you'd like to accomplish. Keep in mind that these goals can apply to you as a team member *and* as an individual athlete. In addition, focusing on realistic, attainable steps at first will give you the confidence and experience to reach for more complex and ambitious goals as you continue your sports journey.

[2]
HYDRATION

No matter how old you are or what sport you play, it's important to stay hydrated. Staying hydrated ensures that your body has enough fluid to function smoothly. Much of our body's hydration comes from the water and other liquids that we drink, but many foods have water content as well—especially fruits and vegetables.

When we're physically active, we sweat and breathe more heavily, both of which deplete our bodies' hydration levels. Because of this, we require additional fluids to replenish what's lost during these activities. Therefore, it's important to hydrate before, during, and after practicing a sport or any type of exercise to avoid the risk of losing too much fluid.

As a young athlete, you'll exert a lot of energy during practice and competitions. This is especially the case in higher temperatures, which can result in even more sweat and loss of fluids. When your body is dehydrated, it shows physical signs of being stressed. These include thirst, dry lips or mouth, headache, feeling queasy or dizzy, and even fever. In addition, being dehydrated can affect your speed and endurance. Water cushions your joints and helps your muscles function, so when you don't have enough liquid in your body, cramps and aches can result.

Children your age can become dehydrated faster than adults, so it's essential to take in enough fluids every day and prepare to drink even more water when you participate in physical activity. Some people prefer sports drinks or other flavored beverages, but watch out for high levels of sugar and other unnecessary ingredients. Ultimately, water is the best choice for athletes of all ages.

Always plan to drink water and stay hydrated before, during, and after exercising. It doesn't matter which sport you play, whether the temperature is hot or cold, or whether you're indoors or outdoors. Make sure you have access to your own personal water bottle or a cooler that you share with your team. You should also try to eat a variety of healthy fruits and vegetables. That way, your body's fluid levels will remain consistent, and your athletic performance will be top notch.

[3]
PROPER
WARM-UPS

One of the most important things to remember is to warm up before you train, practice, or play. This helps prevent injuries by preparing your body for increased physical activity. Since your bones and muscles are continuing to grow and develop, you'll be more likely to get hurt if you don't stretch.

Warming up with careful exercises slowly increases your heart rate and breathing. It also improves your blood flow so that oxygen can travel better throughout your body. Some effective warm-up techniques include walking, jumping jacks, arm circles, and lunges. The goal is to prepare your body by starting slow and working your way up to tougher activities like running.

Warm-up exercises also increase your flexibility, mobility, and overall performance as an athlete. These techniques improve the elasticity and strength of your muscles. By helping the connection between your nerves and muscles, you'll also improve your movement and reaction time. In addition, warming up your body before physical activity prepares your mind to focus on technique and strategy.

[4]
COOL-DOWN
TECHNIQUES

Just as completing a proper warm-up is essential to avoid getting hurt, learning how to cool down after physical activity is vital to your health and performance. Cool-down exercises allow your body to effectively recover from athletic activity, reducing the chance of injury and enhancing your overall health. Cool-down techniques should be performed right after you exercise or participate in a sport. Cooling down encourages your heart rate and blood pressure return to normal, reduces muscle aches and stiffness, and allows your mind and body to relax.

Some effective cool-down exercises include taking a short walk, gentle stretching, and even yoga. Practicing these techniques will allow your circulatory system (heart, blood vessels, and blood) and musculoskeletal system (bones, muscles, cartilage, and connective tissue) to recover from intense activity. They help regulate blood flow and body temperature so that you won't feel stiff and sore the next day.

Cooling down your body also give you the opportunity to calm down mentally and emotionally. Playing a sport often requires intense mental concentration and emotional commitment. As you help your body recover through cool-down exercises, you can also focus on calming their thoughts and feelings. This helps avoid excessive stress and promotes overall health and well-being — after all, your brain is part of your body!

Taking care of yourself as an athlete involves more than just building up athletic skills and focusing on your performance in a particular sport. You also need to think about your long-term physical, mental, and emotional wellness. Allowing yourself to recover after athletic activity will ensure that you have the ability, focus, and positive energy you need for whatever sports you decide to play.

[5]
GOOD
SPORTSMANSHIP

Good sportsmanship is based on the values of respect, fairness, and personal responsibility. When players practice good sportsmanship, they enhance the overall enjoyment and integrity of athletic competition. Some characteristics of good sportsmanship include:

- Abiding by game rules and fair play
- Respecting the authority of coaches, referees, judges, umpires, and other officials
- Encouraging and supporting fellow athletes and teammates
- Giving your personal best
- Accepting losses without blaming or criticizing others

Most people use the term "poor sport" to describe a player who doesn't show good sportsmanship, especially in their reaction to losing a competition. People who are "poor sports" tend to be unnecessarily angry, bitter, or resentful when they lose. This is not only disrespectful, but it also undermines the fun and spirit of healthy competition in sports. Although it can be difficult to lose, it's important to stay true to the values of good sportsmanship.

Sportsmanship is as much about being a good winner as it is about losing with integrity. Of course, it's normal—and healthy—for the winning team and players to be happy about a positive outcome. However, part of being a good sport is to respect your opponent by acting in a kind and considerate way when you win. This means celebrating without being obnoxious, bragging, or rubbing it.

Ultimately, practicing good sportsmanship will not only make your experience better as an athlete, but it will also provide an excellent foundation for how to treat people and behave outside of sports. You'll set a good example for others and be more likely to make friends and form connections with people from all walks of life.

[6]
TEAMWORK

Being involved in sports as a young athlete creates a fantastic opportunity to learn the principles and benefits of teamwork. Whether you're part of a baseball, track, volleyball, or other team, working together with your teammates is a huge part of achieving success. This success includes winning, of course, but it also involves learning how to trust others and work together.

Teams are most effective when everyone is willing to cooperate, collaborate, listen attentively, and put the interests of the group above individual concerns. A valued team member is dependable and supportive, someone who gives their best to help the group succeed. Although each person on a team contributes unique strengths and skills, it's the *collective* efforts of the team that brings powerful results.

Even if you compete in a primarily individual sport, such as martial arts, golf, or gymnastics, there's a good chance that you're still part of a group that must work together for overall success. This includes coaches, sponsors, instructors, officials, and any others who make your participation in the sport possible. Therefore, it's important to remember to treat everyone involved with the sport with respect, abide by the rules, and express gratitude for each person's support when you have the opportunity.

The ability to work toward a goal and positively interact with teammates is a skill that will benefit you well into the future. Not only will you create positive memories of the sport you play, but there's a good chance that you'll also make lasting friendships. Learning how to collaborate effectively and be a team player in sports will help you navigate personal relationships and professional situations to build long-term success and lifetime wins.

[7]
TIME
MANAGEMENT

It can be easy for you to get caught up in the sports you play, especially when it involves a large time commitment to practices, workouts, team meetings, training sessions, and actual play. However, this can take a toll on other areas of your life, including the time and focus you spend on school and academic performance. The good news is that it's possible to balance your athletic and academic success by managing your time efficiently.

Time management is an important life skill for anyone to learn. It involves using the time you have in an efficient and productive way, avoiding distractions, and prioritizing tasks. There are many strategies you can use to organize your time, allowing you to balance academic and athletic commitments. One of these is to keep a detailed schedule for both school and sports. This way, you can view and plan for due dates, exams, practices, games, and spending time with friends. Scheduling regular study and homework sessions each day will help you concentrate on academics so that you can avoid the stress of last-minute cramming.

Some young athletes may think that excelling in school isn't as important as succeeding in sports. The truth is that making education a priority can provide even greater athletic opportunities. In fact, many schools require athletes to be in good academic standing to participate in sports.

Earning good grades and demonstrating a commitment to learning will also improve your chances of attending a college or university with an excellent sports program. That might seem like it's far away, but forming good study habits now will set you up for success as you get closer and closer to your high school graduation. In all cases, learning to manage your time and balance your commitment to both academics *and* sports will provide you with a strong foundation in your athletic, personal, and professional life.

[8]
NUTRITION
AWARENESS

Proper nutrition is important at all ages for athletes and non-athletes alike. However, a healthy diet becomes even more essential during sports season to help you maintain your best athletic performance. Your body receives the essential nutrients it needs—including vitamins, minerals, protein, and calories—from the variety of foods you eat. These nutrients provide the fuel and energy your body needs to function properly. Basically, if your diet is unhealthy or doesn't have enough nutrients, your body won't perform at its best level. As an athlete, this puts you at risk of fatigue, injury, and even illness.

Sometimes it seems easier or more convenient to eat fast food or sugary snacks when you're hungry, especially if you have a busy practice and game schedule. Unfortunately, these foods often contain empty calories and other unhealthy ingredients that can negatively impact your energy levels and performance.

Whenever possible, prepare healthy snacks and simple meals ahead of time so that they're available when you're on the go. For example, you and your family can take a few minutes each weekend to make individual "grab bags" of veggie sticks or fruit slices to keep ready as needed for the week. This will provide you with a nutritious snack option that offers hydration as a bonus.

Overall, it's best to eat a variety of foods to maintain good nutrition. This includes fruits and vegetables, proteins, whole grains, and other nutritious foods. Maintaining healthy and balanced eating habits will lead directly to enhanced athletic performance. Your body will gain the energy and resources that it needs to train, play, grow, and recover effectively. To be sure that you're getting the proper amount of nutrition your body needs, ask your parents or guardians to help. They may even want to schedule a checkup with your family doctor or another medical professional to get their advice.

[9]
REST AND RELAXATION

As an athlete, you put in a great deal of physical work and mental effort, whether you're training, practicing, or playing a sport. That's why rest is essential to allow yourself to physically and mentally recover, as well as replenish your body's energy. Just as it's unhealthy to work or study without breaks, it can be harmful for athletes to participate in their sport every day without some time off.

It can be tempting to push yourself with training and/or practicing every day. However, this is actually counterproductive to your athletic performance—and your health; overtraining in any sport increases the risk of injury, mental fatigue, and physical strain. This can undermine your athletic progress and skill development, making it more difficult to perform at your best.

Appreciating the importance of rest and recovery as an athlete means you keep your muscles flexible and allow them to repair in order to build strength. In addition, regular downtime away from your sport will improve the quality of your sleep and mental focus. Taking time to rest and recover from *any* activity is beneficial for your health and overall well-being, and this includes athletics. Regular breaks from intense, consistent athletic activity will not only maximize your development and performance, but it will also help you balance your other commitments and renew your enthusiasm for playing sports.

[10]
INJURY
PREVENTION

Injuries often cause physical pain in addition to interrupting an athlete's participation in sports. Many sports injuries are short term and heal quickly without too many lasting effects. However, even young athletes can suffer serious injuries that require intense treatment and long-term rehabilitation.

Sadly, some sports-related injuries can be devastating, leaving athletes impaired, in pain, or even permanently disabled. Although it's likely that you'll get a few bruises or scrapes while playing your sport, using the right techniques can minimize the risk and protect against more serious physical harm.

Effective warm-up and cool-down exercises and staying hydrated are essential ways to preventing injuries. In addition, wearing recommended protective gear related to the sport you play is an excellent way to minimize the risk of getting injured. These may include a helmet, pads, guards, gloves, and shoes that support your ankle.

Perhaps the most important aspect of preventing a sports injury is listening to your body. Sometimes, athletes are under the impression that they should "walk it off" or ignore pain or discomfort. Unfortunately, this can lead to more severe harm in the long run, especially if it's a serious problem like hitting your head or having chest pain. No athletic event or competition is worth a serious injury or long-term disability. Therefore, if you feel any pain or sense that something is physically wrong during an athletic activity, be sure to tell a coach, official, or parent immediately.

It's especially important for young athletes to take the risk of injury seriously — not just so they can continue to play sports but also for their overall health and long-term wellness. Learning ways to prevent injury and taking precautions to keep your body safe are fundamental to enjoying a fulfilling sports journey and lifelong physical activity.

[11]
MINDSET
MATTERS

Most athletes would agree that playing any sport involves as much mental effort as physical work. Therefore, your mindset truly matters when it comes to athletics. The more positive you feel about yourself and your talents, the more positive your experience will be within the sport you play. This positivity will enhance your success as an athlete and in other areas of life.

It can be difficult for players to mentally cope with disappointing outcomes. This can include an individual or team loss, experiencing an injury, or just feeling that your performance wasn't "good enough." Instead of dwelling on disappointment, it's far healthier to realize that the past can't be changed and focus on the future with a positive outlook—whether that means the next game, competition, or season. Learning from your experiences as you move forward builds a resilient mindset for success. Resilience helps you recover from setbacks and regain your confidence after making a mistake.

Keep in mind that cultivating a positive and resilient mindset doesn't mean that you won't ever experience negative emotions about certain aspects of your athletic journey. However, this approach ensures that you can face setbacks, rebound, and still have fun while playing your sport. This mindset will also lead you to future success in all areas of life, from sports to relationships to careers and beyond.

[12]
PERFORMANCE PRESSURE

Even at a young age, you might have already felt pressure to perform. These pressures can range from your personal expectations to external expectations—whether real or perceived—from parents, coaches, and teammates. To cope with performance pressure, it's important to develop healthy strategies that will help you maintain perspective and support your love of sports.

Everyone has a little voice inside that's capable of both criticism and encouragement. To avoid putting extreme pressure on yourself as an athlete, it's vital to keep this voice as positive as possible. If your self-talk turns harsh or negative, take a moment to remember that you deserve to be treated with kindness and respect—especially by yourself!

Another strategic method for coping with internal performance pressure is to avoid comparing yourself to other players—no matter whether it's someone on your team, an opponent, or a professional athlete. It may sound cliché, but all you can do is put forth your best effort, and that's enough.

Sometimes, parents, coaches, and even teammates don't realize the pressure they put on a player. They may believe that high expectations of performance or expressions of "tough love" are good forms of motivation, but this doesn't work for all players. To maintain your perspective and positivity toward the sport you play, a good strategy is to focus on the current moment and just do your best. Don't get stuck on previous outcomes or what anyone had to say about them, just as you should avoid worrying about outcomes in the future. Nobody is perfect when it comes to athletics, so no one should expect perfection in sports.

If you notice that you're under more pressure to perform than you can handle, or if you're feeling anxiety related to playing sports, let a trusted adult—such as a parent or coach—know so that they can provide you with support. Athletics is a great way to learn skills, meet people, and develop new strengths, but sports should ultimately be *fun*, not a source of anxiety or stress. If performance pressure is affecting your overall enjoyment, then something needs to change.

[13]
PROPER
TECHNIQUE

Each sport has its own fundamental techniques of play and competition. For example, soccer is fundamentally based on kicking and passing the ball among your teammates toward the opponent's goal and defending your team's goal to prevent the opposing team from scoring. Although you may enjoy certain aspects of a sport more than others—or decide to focus on just one athletic area or skill set—it's still helpful to learn all the rules and positions. This will improve your contribution as an individual sports competitor *and* as part of a team.

There are many team sports that are divided into player positions such as offense and defense, making it difficult to learn all the specific skills necessary for each. However, even if you play a certain position on a team, it's important to understand the overall basics of the sport. This will enhance your athletic knowledge and performance, in addition to giving you an appreciation for the efforts of your teammates and the sport as a whole.

To be sure that you master the fundamental techniques of your sport properly, you'll need to learn relevant and basic rules, skills, and strategies. You can improve your athletic knowledge and understanding by reading about your sport, watching professionals play, and even talking with your coaches and fellow team members. Paying close attention during practice and training can also give you an overall understanding and appreciation of the sport you play, no matter which position you're assigned.

[14]
STRENGTH TRAINING

Physical strength is a big part of most sports, which is why it's essential for young athletes to understand age-appropriate strength training and its benefits. Strength training is not the same as lifting weights or building muscles; in fact, any form of heavy weightlifting can result in serious injury for athletes who are still growing and developing. Instead, strength training involves the safe use of light weights with controlled movements and proper form. It's a beneficial way to improve your sports technique and overall health.

Strength training can also protect against injury. It promotes fitness, strong bones, and a healthy cardiovascular system. Rather than using weights or machines, you can use your own body weight for exercises that build strength. Some examples include push-ups, lunges, squats, pull-ups, and any activity in which your body weight provides resistance.

Before beginning any strength-training program, be sure to learn proper techniques, exercises, and forms. If you're not sure who else to ask, start by talking to your coach or a gym teacher. This way, you can avoid injuries like muscle strains and joint problems. Keep in mind that the goal of this type of training is to strengthen your muscles and overall physical fitness, not to put yourself at risk by lifting heavy weights.

[15]
FLEXIBILITY
TRAINING

Many sports require physical flexibility so that an athlete's body can move properly. For example, gymnasts develop high flexibility to ensure their range of motion is sufficient to perform impressive skills and routines. In addition, flexibility enhances agility, which is the ability to move quickly and easily. Flexibility training, when done correctly, can improve your overall athletic skill, as well as help prevent injury and decrease muscle stiffness and soreness.

Many people associate stretching with flexibility training. Stretches can certainly increase the range of motion for your muscles, enhance blood flow, and improve your agility. Stretching is especially important for muscles such as calves, hip flexors, quadriceps, and hamstrings. Flexibility training and stretching exercises can be done during warm-up and cool-down periods. Some examples of flexibility training include different types of lunges, seat straddles, and quad stretches.

Like all training exercises, it's best to consult a professional about flexibility training to be sure you have the right form and approach. This will help you avoid injury and maximize your agility. If you experience any swelling or pain, though, you should stop stretching immediately. In addition, it's important not to overuse your muscles by training too much or focusing too hard on one group of muscles.

[16]
BALANCE
TRAINING

Developing balance is essential for everyday life, but it's especially important for athletes. Balance training improves muscle strength and steadiness, which allows for better physical control when playing sports. Incorporating balance exercises in your athletic training will enhance your stability and overall performance on the field, court, mat, or wherever you play.

The human balance system involves your sense of sight, organs within your inner ear, and sensory signals from your muscles, tendons, and joints. These elements work together to provide your brain with information about the position of your body as it relates to your environment. This allows your brain to adjust to gravity and other outside forces. You might notice, for example, that the way you balance changes when walking on a sandy beach compared to a concrete sidewalk. Balance training can improve the way this system works so that your brain can correctly interpret information and react quickly, keeping your body aligned as it moves.

There are many balance exercises that you can do almost anywhere. Some of these include standing on one leg while slightly lifting the other, then alternating; walking heel to toe (as if on a tightrope); and doing knee lifts and different squats. Tai chi and yoga routines are also excellent ways to strengthen your balance with the added benefits of flexibility and mindfulness. There are also several benefits to training in a pool since you're not only working against gravity but also the changing movement of the water around you. In addition, exercising the body's core muscles, including the abdominals and those that attach to the spine, enhances your overall stability and athletic skills.

[17]
SPEED
TRAINING

Success in many sports depends on a player's speed. These sports might involve running, swimming, or skating. An athlete's speed can be an advantage in overall performance while also improving agility, muscle power, and range of motion. This means you'll be able to accelerate, change direction, and physically respond to outside forces with quick reflexes.

Many targeted drills can improve your physical speed. These include sprint drills, wall runs, power jumps and/or skips, and arm swings/drives. Depending on the sport you play, your speed training may include different exercises to target specific movements related to your position or mode of competition. To avoid injury during speed training, be sure to consult your coach or trainer on the proper form and movement necessary for each drill.

Another important part of speed training is improving reaction time. The faster a player can process an action and respond, the better their ability to play sports as a whole. For example, a baseball player with quick reaction time is likely to be an asset in fielding balls, throwing, and making plays at the bases.

Certain strategies can improve your reaction time depending on the sport you play. Carefully practicing repetitive actions such as catching, throwing, and kicking can develop muscle memory and quick reflexes. Watching professional athletes can also give you ideas for ways to respond rapidly on the field, court, or wherever you play.

[18]
ENDURANCE

One way to achieve success as an athlete is to develop stamina and build endurance. Stamina is the strength to continue doing something challenging. For example, cyclists in the Tour de France demonstrate an incredible amount of stamina as they ride for miles each day across various terrain in hot weather.

Athletes develop physical stamina through practice and training. Mental stamina is important for athletes as well, especially in sports that require deep concentration for long periods of time. Endurance is similar to stamina in that it defines a person's ability to keep going in the face of stressful, adverse, or extended conditions. For example, an athlete must have a tremendous amount of endurance to complete a triathlon.

You can develop stamina and endurance through training and practice. Setting goals to increase the intensity or duration of activity will improve your physical and mental stamina. For example, if you want to develop your running stamina, you might increase your distance by a few yards each week or try to increase your speed by a few seconds.

Overall, the more effective your methods to increase your physical and mental stamina, the greater your endurance and athletic skills will be. These traits allow you to persevere when faced with athletic challenges, as well as grow your individual strength and power as a competitor.

[19]
POWER GENERATION

In addition to speed, strength, flexibility, balance, and endurance, many sports require strength of movement for success. This may include the ability to powerfully throw, kick, or hit a ball; execute a wrestling or tackle move; or complete a pole vault or long jump. Generating power in athletic movement usually means creating the maximum amount of force with great speed.

Training exercises can help increase your power in athletic movements, especially in relation to speed and strength training. These two strategies apply strength to energetic, quick movement as a means of generating power. Breathing exercises can also develop your body's power, allowing more oxygen to reach your muscles and prevent strains. Additional exercises include specific jumps, lifts, and sprints.

There are also other considerations such as accuracy and precision that athletes need to be successful. For example, while it's great to be a powerful kicker in football, that skill wouldn't help much if you can only kick the ball in one direction. Therefore, power training should be balanced with proper technique and the specific skills associated with the sport you play.

[20]
FUNDAMENTALS

As previously mentioned, it's important for athletes to know and understand the basics associated with whichever sport they play. This includes mastering general concepts, strategies, and athletic skills, as well as developing an overall appreciation for the sport itself. Another fundamental of sports you should prioritize as a young athlete is learning and applying the basic rules and regulations of play and competition.

When athletes focus on the fundamental rules and regulations of their sport, it improves their athletic performance and overall sportsmanship. For example, understanding what constitutes a foul in basketball or a penalty in football can help players avoid those actions and their consequences. Abiding by the rules of play also helps competitors act responsibly toward their teammates and remain respectful of opponents and officials.

There are always opportunities to learn more about the foundation, rules, and regulations for the sport that you play through reading, watching others compete, and adhering to the directions of trainers, coaches, and officials. Prioritizing an understanding of the fundamentals of your sport is just as important as developing your athletic skills. Knowing the basics allows you to process how to be a productive and dependable player who demonstrates good sportsmanship.

[21]
ADAPTABILITY

Adaptability is the ability to adjust to new situations and conditions. This quality allows you to navigate uncertainty and react to unfamiliar scenarios. As a young athlete, you're likely to face many scenarios that require you to adapt, whether it's new teammates, a different coach, playing an unfamiliar position, or facing a variety of opponents. Being adaptable will help you make the necessary adjustments to maintain your athletic performance and continue enjoying your sport.

It's important to understand as much as possible about what the season may entail for each sport, in addition to individual games or meets. This encourages realistic expectations as well as adaptability. For example, certain sports are played no matter the weather — rain, snow, or extremely warm conditions.

In addition, many sports feature "away" games or meets that require travel and involve competing in new environments against unfamiliar opponents with unique strategies. Athletes must also adjust to changes such as going into overtime or switching a lineup even while on their home turf.

Learning to adapt is an essential skill that can be applied to many aspects of life as well as athletics. When young athletes are prepared to face different game scenarios and opponents, they'll have a much easier time adapting to unusual or challenging situations. If you notice that you're having difficulty adapting to unfamiliar circumstances, reach out to your coach or other players; they may have tips to share that will help you adjust more easily.

[22]
EFFECTIVE
COMMUNICATION

The success of many team sports depends on communication among the players, on and off the field. Even individual sports require communication between the competing athlete and their coach, along with judges, officials, and event coordinators. Communication is based on sharing and understanding information with mutual respect on both sides of the exchange. Effective communication builds a positive sports environment, reduces misunderstandings and conflict, and allows everyone to contribute toward reaching shared goals.

When you're on the field or wherever you actively play, it's important to communicate clearly with your teammates or coaches. For example, football players must communicate about which play will be run so that they can coordinate their positions and movements on the field. Many sports rely on nonverbal communication strategies as well, such as hand signals and other cues. For instance, you can see this pattern of communication in baseball between the catcher and the pitcher.

When you exchange information clearly and effectively with your teammates and others involved in your sport, you build trust and understanding. This allows everyone to work together and function as a unit rather than as individual players.

Communication among teammates is also important off the field when you aren't actively playing your sport. Showing genuine respect and care for your fellow players in words and actions will encourage strong bonds and unity. Make sure your interactions are truthful and positive whenever possible to create a supportive environment where you all stick together as a team. Of course, you'll still have a few hiccups every once in a while, but effective communication will help you and others involved in your sport navigate these issues without letting them become a permanent problem.

[23]
RESILIENCE

When you feel passionately about something, it can be more difficult to handle setbacks when they occur. One common setback in sports is injury; any athletic activity has some risk of injury, ranging from minor bumps and bruises to more serious trauma like broken bones, concussions, and muscle tears.

Unfortunately, some injuries can interrupt an athlete's season or even end their participation in a sport altogether. This type of setback can be very hard to overcome, even with a strong foundation of resilience. That's why it's important to have a balanced lifestyle between sports and other activities.

When it comes to resilience, people often mention strategies such as positive thinking, mindfulness, having purpose, and practicing self-care. These are all important aspects of resilience as a characteristic that can help you bounce back from disappointment. However, one element of resilience in athletes that is sometimes overlooked is mental preparation and a realistic perspective.

This isn't to say that you should always expect the worst or anticipate major setbacks. However, keeping your expectations realistic and balancing your relationships, hobbies, and other passions along with dedication to your sport will help you overcome disappointments when they do happen.

In truth, only a few athletes make it on the varsity team in high school or play for college. There are many opportunities for fulfillment in life, and playing a sport is just one of them. The key is to keep an open mind and invest in activities that bring you happiness outside of sports. That way, you'll have other pursuits to fall back on in case of injury or other interruptions. The more realistic your perspective about the role athletics will play during your lifetime, the more resilient you'll be in the face of potential setbacks as a player.

[24]
SELF-REFLECTION

Young athletes often look for outward confirmation of their performance in sports. This makes sense, especially considering the heavy influence of numbers and statistics in athletics overall. Scores show who won — and by how much — as well as individual records and levels of competitive performance. Feedback from your coaches, trainers, teammates, and even spectators can also provide you with a sense of whether you're meeting or exceeding expectations as a player. These external factors can be good sources of motivation for you to continue improving and doing your best.

However, it's also important to practice self-reflection as a young athlete. This gives you the chance to look at how you're performing and how you feel about it. For example, you might be happy with your ranking as above average even if your performance doesn't meet the expectations of other players who want to be number one. There's nothing wrong with playing a sport just to have fun.

Don't forget to think about academics as well. After all, your education is what will lead to advancements in your future. Self-reflection will allow you to feel pride in your performance even if you aren't considered the "best" athlete in your sport. Your internal values will help you measure your athletic success on your own terms.

Self-reflection can also help you figure out how to improve and accomplish your personal goals. For example, you may realize that you can improve your free throws with more practice or finding ways to refine your technique. Once you know this, you can plan steps toward achieving that goal.

Being able to assess your own performance — not just in sports but in all areas of life — presents you with opportunities for growth and self-fulfillment. It can also keep you motivated and inspired to set goals and succeed.

[25]
MISTAKES AND LOSSES

Everyone makes mistakes, from new athletes to the most experienced and talented professionals. Mistakes can occur at any time, especially in sports where multiple things are happening at once. Errors are common and usually a result of misjudgment or lack of knowledge. Sometimes, you might feel you've let others down or caused a loss, which only leads to unhealthy thoughts. A much better approach when dealing with mistakes is to embrace and learn from them.

In athletics — and life in general — mistakes are an opportunity to learn. When you're new to a sport, you're probably still learning the rules and required skills. Making a mistake allows you to examine what went wrong and how you can improve in the future. Even if you have years of experience playing a sport, it's likely that you'll make errors at times. For example, you may miss a pass or a catch that might've seemed easy to observers. However, it's important to learn that no one is perfect. This attitude can also make you more forgiving toward others when they make a mistake in the middle of a game.

Dwelling on your mistakes can actually have negative effects on your athletic performance. For example, continuing to think about a missed catch or shot will interrupt your focus and likely cause you to miss the next one as well, creating a cycle of unwanted outcomes. Overthinking about a mistake you made, no matter how recently, is unhealthy because it can keep your mind trapped in that moment.

If you find yourself preoccupied with an error, acknowledge that it happened and actively shift your thinking to the present, focusing on what you're doing *now*. Ultimately, any mistakes you might have made have already happened, and nobody can go back and change the past! However, you *do* have the opportunity to learn from your mistakes, move on, and try to do better next time.

[26]
MENTAL
TOUGHNESS

There is no doubt that participating in athletics requires physical toughness in the form of strength, endurance, and diligent training. In most sports, mental toughness is often just as important as the physical kind. Even young athletes must put in a great deal of concentration, learning, and mental effort for their sports. By strengthening your mind just as you would your body, you'll be prepared for challenging situations in all areas of life.

One way to develop your mental toughness is to stay focused on the present and maintain a healthy perspective. For example, it can be difficult to tune out the crowd when you know your friends and loved ones are watching you play. Training yourself to focus on the present can keep you from getting nervous or distracted.

Maintaining a healthy perspective is another aspect of mental toughness that involves positive thinking. There's no doubt that sports, competitions, and individual athletic performance are important; however, these things are just smaller parts of your overall life. If you lose a game, it doesn't mean you're a bad person or that you won't be able to pass your quiz in math.

Strengthening your mental toughness allows you to focus on your goals and the steps to reach them, in addition to helping you overcome any setbacks. Mental toughness is related to positive thinking, which provides you with the tools to interrupt negative self-talk and develop a more optimistic mindset when facing challenging situations both on and off the field.

[27]
RULES AND REGULATIONS

As with any game or competition, you'll be a better player when you know and understand the rules of your sport. Even if you think certain regulations may not apply to the position you play or your level of competition, it's still good to have a general sense of the overall guidelines related to the sport you enjoy.

Some sports have more complex rules than others, especially those that involve multiple players and positions such as football, hockey, and baseball. However, it's important to keep in mind that you don't need to learn everything right away. You'll start out with the basics and then learn more about advanced regulations as you gain more experience.

There are several effective strategies to help you become well-versed in the rules of your sport. One of the most important of these is to pay close attention and listen to your coach when they are giving instructions, explanations, and directions. Reading up on the rules of your sport, watching professionals play, and asking questions of more experienced players can also provide a deeper understanding of the rules and regulations.

Knowing and following the rules of your sport will allow you to avoid any personal infractions or team penalties, which can negatively affect the outcome of a competition. For example, if you're an expert in the rules of soccer, you'll be less likely to earn a penalty for a handball, being offsides, or other player misconduct. Familiarity with your sport's regulations will also ensure that you practice good sportsmanship by demonstrating respect for your team, coaches, and the officials.

[28]
REFEREE
RESPECT

Referees, umpires, and other athletic officials are an essential part of almost every sport. Without them, athletic events would be chaotic and almost impossible to manage. Their job is to enforce the rules of play and oversee a fair competition with good sportsmanship. Officials learn the rules and regulations so that they can ensure the safety of participants and make sure each match is properly conducted.

You can show respect to referees, umpires, and officials by following the rules, listening to their instructions, and accepting their decisions without complaint or displays of anger. As an individual athlete, you should maintain your composure and respect regardless of how *others* behave, including fellow teammates and spectators. Respect for sports officials should be practiced at all times. This means avoiding negative comments or attitudes toward officials, whether you're in the locker room, a team meeting, or anywhere else.

It's important to remember that sports officials are human and deserving of personal and professional respect. They agree to be impartial, meaning that they won't favor any specific team, player, or coach. Although mistakes can happen, these officials have the final word of authority in determining fairness and accuracy in athletic competition. Respecting their decisions is a significant part of good sportsmanship and decency, even if you disagree with their call.

Ultimately, officiating athletic competition can feel like a necessary but thankless job. No matter what, *someone* is sure to be disappointed with the outcome. Keep this in mind as a young athlete, and take the opportunity when you can to thank referees and officials for your sport.

[29]
STAYING
HUMBLE

When an individual athlete or team wins a competition, it's natural for them to celebrate their success. In fact, most televised sports feature huge celebrations for the winners, from ceremonies at the Olympics to confetti across the Super Bowl field. Winning players are often interviewed about their success amid these celebrations, and it can be difficult even for professional players to stay humble in those moments. However, humility is a key characteristic for successful athletes who have a true love of sports.

Being humble shows that you have a sense of modesty about your success instead of being arrogant. For example, if someone compliments you on a great athletic play, you can thank them without bragging. The opposite of a humble response in this case might be giving a play-by-play recap of what happened or putting others down to make yourself look better. This doesn't mean that you shouldn't celebrate your victories; instead, practicing humility is about being considerate of people's feelings. You can recognize your own accomplishments without hurting someone else's feelings.

Humility is especially important for athletes when they're members of a team. Certain positions in various sports seem to stand out or receive more attention than others, such as the quarterback in football, the pitcher in softball, and the goalie in soccer. However, no matter the position you play on a team, staying humble about your performance will foster respect and goodwill among your teammates. Your humility will also set a good example for others who look up to you on the team.

[30]
DIVERSITY AND INCLUSION

One of the benefits of playing sports is the opportunity to meet people from different backgrounds who share your athletic interests and a common goal of forming a successful team. Just as you wouldn't want your team to be made up of members who play the same position, you shouldn't want your team members to be identical to each other either. A diverse team is made up of people with different experiences, cultures, appearances, and skill sets.

Sometimes, people have negative reactions to things that are unfamiliar based on what they know and understand. Appreciating diversity means keeping an open mind about someone without making any judgments. This includes a person's identity, background, culture, appearance, and anything else that makes them who they are. When it comes to your teammates, you can show your appreciation by treating them with respect and communicating in a sincere and positive manner.

Be sure to avoid any stereotypes by acknowledging each person as a unique and valuable individual. This shows support for your fellow players and encourages harmony and unity within your team as a whole, leading to a more rewarding experience for everyone. Respecting and embracing diversity within your athletic team allows you to open your heart and mind to new friendships that can last beyond the sports season.

The more diversity among your teammates, the more chances you have of learning about other cultures, traditions, and perspectives. This will not only broaden your knowledge of the world, but it will also provide opportunities for you to improve your social skills and how you relate to different people now and in the future.

[31]
OFF-SEASON
TRAINING

Most organized sports take place in a season, meaning there are a certain number of weeks in each year of official competition. For example, a regular football season typically begins in late summer or early fall and ends in late November (or very early December). A sports season may last a few weeks longer for those who make it to the playoffs or championship games. Once the season is finished, however, players usually don't spend any official time participating in the sport until the next season begins. This period is known as the off-season.

The off-season is a great opportunity for athletes to participate in focused training on their own. This may include developing existing skills, learning new athletic techniques, practicing to gain more experience, or building overall speed, strength, and endurance. You can work at your own pace in the off-season and be more relaxed in structuring your training without the pressures that come with competition. You can also invite teammates to train with you as a way of staying in touch and continue working together. However, it's important to train properly and safely to avoid any injuries that might prevent you from participating in your sport when the off-season is finished.

Of course, taking mental and physical breaks is also important. During the competitive season, these breaks are likely to be short and in between games, practices, and meets. However, the off-season allows for more frequent and lengthy breaks from training and practicing. More time off can help you avoid over-training and athletic burnout.

Finding a balance between focused training and time away from your sport in the off-season is the best strategy for maintaining your athletic skills, allowing your mind and body to rest and remain healthy, which prepares you to enjoy the next season of competition.

[32]
SPORTSMANSHIP
IN VICTORY

Occasionally, athletes get so caught up in winning a game or event that they forget the principles of good sportsmanship. This can lead to arrogant or even obnoxious behavior like bragging or rubbing it in to opponents. Aside from demonstrating a lack of good sportsmanship, this behavior reflects badly on coaches, other teammates, and the organizations sponsoring the sport itself. That's why winning graciously and with humility is important; it ensures that everyone remains respectful and has a good experience.

There are many ways to celebrate a sports win with grace and humility. For example, you always thank your opponents for a good competition whenever you have the opportunity. Showing your appreciation for the officials involved is also a way to win graciously and demonstrate your respect for the spirit of your sport.

Once you're away from spectators and competitors, you can freely express your pride and excitement in victory. However, this should never include negativity toward anyone else, especially the opposing side.

Essentially, sportsmanship in victory is based on respect for everyone involved, as well as the sport itself. It's important to remember that no athlete or team ends up on the winning side every time. Therefore, when you win, you should behave with good sportsmanship and thoughtfulness, just as you'd hope others do when they win.

[33]
RECOVERY STRATEGIES

As a young athlete, your body may bounce back quickly even from strenuous training sessions, practices, and competitions. However, just because you don't experience aches, pains, and soreness right after playing your sport doesn't mean that your body won't benefit from recovery strategies. In fact, it may take time for your body to show signs of wear and tear due to overtraining and over-conditioning. Therefore, implementing various recovery techniques will enhance your overall health and wellness in addition to your athletic skills so that you can perform at an optimal level in the future.

All athletes require physical recovery. This means giving yourself time to rest just after and between athletic activities. Short-term recovery strategies help your body return to a normal state after exercise. Your heart and breathing rates also slow down at an appropriate pace through cool-down exercises and low-intensity activities. Properly cooling off helps with muscle soreness and injury prevention.

Long-term recovery in sports involves a greater duration of rest between periods of athletic activity, such as a weekend or seasonal break. Resting keeps your body from becoming fatigued and prevents long-term injuries. This will improve your overall performance when you return to play.

Athletes also require mental recovery. Playing a sport demands a great deal of concentration and focus. Taking time away from athletics allows you to participate in other activities and clear your mind. It also creates opportunities to balance your lifestyle so that your sport doesn't overtake other important aspects of your life, such as spending time with family, having fun with friends, studying, and taking part in other hobbies.

Keeping the importance of recovery in mind will prevent injury, burnout, and other factors that can interfere with playing sports. Using recovery techniques as a young athlete is a way to ensure your performance and enjoyment remain strong over the course of your athletic career.

[34]
TIME MANAGEMENT

Ask any athlete, whether amateur or professional, and they'll tell you that time is one of the biggest commitments for playing a sport. On top of that, you probably have additional pressures and commitments such as academics, extracurricular activities, and social obligations. Your family will need commit some of their time as well to address things like scheduling, transportation, and team meetings. Because of this, it's important to get a realistic sense of the time required for participating in a sport (on everyone's part) before you commit to playing.

If you find that you can't commit to the time required for the sport you want to play, keep in mind that there are other options you can pursue. Many community centers offer temporary sports camps or informal games that take place after school, on weekends, and during school breaks. You can also gather a group of friends to play a "pick-up" game of basketball, soccer, softball, or your choice of sport at a local park when it's convenient.

Another way to stay engaged in a sport without a formal time commitment is to learn about it or modify it to play as an individual. This may include watching professionals play, reading up on the history of your sport, or safely practicing certain moves and training to build your athletic skills.

If you are able to commit to the time required for your sport, be sure that you do so in good faith. In other words, be responsible, consistent, and engaged when training, practicing, and competing. Showing up on time and putting forth your best effort will help you get the most out of the experience as a young athlete and demonstrate good character to your fellow players. In addition, fulfilling your time commitment to sports will foster perseverance, dedication, and focus—characteristics that will benefit you throughout your athletic and personal life.

[35]
THE IMPORTANCE OF SLEEP

More than ever, experts are realizing the importance of quality sleep for overall health and well-being, no matter a person's age. An interrupted or irregular sleep schedule can result in fatigue, lack of focus, unhealthy coping behaviors (such as consuming excessive sugar and caffeine), mood changes, and reduced performance in daily activities. These can have especially negative consequences for young athletes, as you need more sleep when you're still growing to maintain physical and mental wellness.

Young athletes often have busy schedules due to training, practices, and games or competitions. When you factor in academics and other activities, it can be difficult to keep a regular bedtime routine during the week and get enough quality sleep. However, sleep disruption and deprivation can actually change your body's natural rhythm, making it even more difficult to fall and stay asleep when you're tired.

Some people believe they can catch up on their sleep deficit by waking up later on weekends or sleeping in on holidays. Unfortunately, the amount of sleep you miss builds up during the week, making it unlikely that you'll be able to make it up with extra sleep on Saturday or Sunday.

Prioritizing sufficient, quality sleep is just as essential as maintaining a healthy diet and proper athletic training. It reduces your chances of injury and illness in addition to making sure you're at your physical and mental best for your sport. Be sure to implement a calm and consistent bedtime routine and, though it may be hard, avoid the use of any screens at least an hour before going to sleep. The blue light from devices like tablets and phones can signal to your brain that it's time to wake up. Instead, use that time for reading, journaling, meditation, or another relaxing activity. This will prepare your mind and body for a good night's sleep so that you can wake up feeling restored and rejuvenated.

[36]
BALANCED
LIFESTYLE

Playing a sport, whether as an individual or part of a team, can be one of the most rewarding and exciting activities at any age. As you gain experience and develop your skills, playing sports may become an even bigger part of who you are. However, while it's admirable to be dedicated to athletic activities, it's essential to keep a balanced lifestyle so that your sport doesn't overshadow other priorities such as personal interests and relationships with family and friends.

Even as a young athlete, you likely know that participating in a sport requires a big commitment of time and energy. However, there are other aspects of your personal life that deserve your time and energy as well. One of the most important of these is your relationships with your family and friends outside of sports. Make sure you spend quality time with them away from any athletic activities. This will strengthen your bonds and remind you that people love you for who you are, not because you're a skilled athlete.

Another essential part of your personal life you must balance with sports is other hobbies and interests. Allow yourself to pursue and enjoy activities that have nothing to do with athletics, such as art, music, and reading. This gives you the opportunity to expand your knowledge and keep growing as a person.

Overall, maintaining a balance between sports and your personal life is essential for your health, relationships, and well-being. If you notice that athletics are interfering with your academic success, hobbies, or personal relationships, it might be time to adjust your focus and rebalance your lifestyle. Take intentional breaks from your sport, and plan to do something fun with the most important people in your life. You can also catch up on homework to improve your academic grades or devote some of your time and energy to a volunteer opportunity that inspires you. You'll appreciate the fulfillment of a well-balanced life.

[37]
MENTORSHIP

A mentor is someone you trust who has experience in a certain area and can offer advice and guidance. When it comes to sports, players often find valuable mentors in their coaches and other experienced athletes. These individuals can support you in setting goals, enhancing your performance, and making decisions about your future as an athlete.

Your coach can give you guidance and advice about your sport in general and for you as an individual. This may include specific pointers for proper form, skills relevant to your position, and other athletic strategies. More experienced athletes can also give you advice, as well as model good sportsmanship and inspire a positive, winning spirit.

In addition to providing you with guidance and advice about the sport you play, coaches and fellow athletes can also serve as mentors for other aspects of your life. They often have expertise in leadership, self-discipline, and other traits that lead to success. In addition, they've likely experienced and overcome challenges — on and off the field — making them role models for perseverance and helpful life skills.

Although it may feel intimidating at first to approach your coach or a fellow athlete, you can start by asking some easy questions when it's a convenient time for them. For example, you may decide to volunteer your time after a game to organize equipment or help with another task, which gives you the chance to ask for some simple advice. You'll be able to gradually establish a mentor relationship in addition to demonstrating your interest and dedication. As you build associations with coaches and athletes, you'll benefit from their wisdom, support, and guidance. Be sure to express your gratitude for their willingness to share their insights.

[38]
HEALTHY
HABITS

Maintaining good hygiene involves taking measures to keep your body, belongings, and environment as clean as possible. This promotes health and prevents illness, but it also makes everything more pleasant for those are around you. Playing sports often requires intense physical activity, which can lead to sweaty athletes, stinky uniforms and protective gear, and dirty equipment. Therefore, it's especially important for athletes to practice good hygiene for their personal health and that of their fellow players, in addition to maintaining team respect and harmony.

There are a few key strategies for athletes when it comes to good personal hygiene. This includes keeping your body clean with a daily bathing or shower routine, maintaining dental health by brushing and flossing your teeth, and washing your hands properly with soap and water after using the restroom. Many athletes also benefit from using deodorant to reduce sweat and body odor. Those who wear sports uniforms or any type of athletic attire for games, training, and practice should ensure that they are thoroughly cleaned after each use. In addition, if you have any symptoms of illness, staying home to rest and recover will ensure that your teammates aren't exposed to anything contagious.

In athletics, it's also important to take pride in the cleanliness of your equipment and surroundings. For example, you may have a locker in your school gym where you keep your gear and other necessities. Keeping your locker, equipment, and the surrounding area clean and tidy will demonstrate respect toward your fellow players. This also applies to shared spaces where you practice and/or play. Be sure to properly dispose of any trash and take good care of team equipment. Doing your part to maintain your personal hygiene, as well as contribute to a positive environment for your team, will carry you far in sports and beyond.

[39]
PERSONAL BOUNDARIES

Participating in any type of athletics involves a commitment of time and effort, and most players find their sports to be a rewarding and enjoyable experience overall. However, you may not realize the potentially negative effects that come with a long-term commitment to athletics. Occasionally, young athletes need help in setting boundaries so that they don't over-commit to their sport, putting their other obligations, health, or relationships at risk.

Your coaches, trainers, and teammates should understand and support you in making sure you have adequate time and resources for success in school. In fact, some schools will not allow you to participate in sports if your grades drop below a certain level. In college sports, you could even lose your scholarship if you don't pass your classes.

If you need to set limits for your participation in athletics to study for an exam, catch up on homework, or attend tutoring sessions, be sure to speak to your coach as soon as possible so that the problem doesn't become worse. You might be able to reduce your commitment in some way, whether with practices, traveling to away games, or other aspects of your sport. Use that time to focus on restoring your good status in academics.

Another healthy boundary to consider for your sports commitment is how it may affect your family members. Participation in athletics often comes with a financial commitment that can get quite expensive with player fees, uniforms, equipment, and transportation. A good strategy for setting boundaries in this case is to check in with your parent or guardian and make sure that they're financially prepared before you sign up for any athletic extras such as training camps, travel teams, or additional sports.

It's also important to consider the time commitment to your sport and how that might affect your family — including your siblings — and their schedules. Open communication with your family will allow you to establish healthy boundaries so that your sports commitment doesn't have negative effects on your relationships and home life.

[40]
POSITIVE
VISUALIZATION

One successful performance strategy used by many athletes is positive visualization. This technique can improve your athletic skills by training your brain and your nervous system to visualize an outcome you want to have in real life. Positive visualization helps you stay motivated and focused on achieving your goals. It can also strengthen the belief you have in yourself and encourage you to take advantage of opportunities in the future.

Visualization means forming specific mental images of yourself completing different actions that help you achieve a goal. For example, if you play golf, you might use positive visualization before you begin at each hole. This may include imagining a fluid swing or putting a ball right into the cup. If you happen to be a gymnast, you may visualize yourself performing each part of a routine with precision and skill.

Of course, visualization is not a replacement for developing and practicing your actual skills. However, forming these mental images of success can calm your nerves and reduce anxiety before you participate in any athletic event, which will help you perform at your best.

The best place to practice visualization is somewhere quiet where you won't be disturbed. You can do this for a few seconds or up to a couple of minutes. Most people close their eyes, focus, and breathe deeply as they imagine each step toward achieving their desired outcome. It also helps to form clear and detailed images in your mind to make the experience feel as real as possible. The more you practice positive visualization, the easier and more effective it becomes.

You can use this technique beyond sports to reduce stress and improve performance in situations such as taking an exam, learning to drive, or trying out for the school play. Overall, positive visualization is a valuable mental exercise that will enhance your performance, ease anxiety, and motivate you for success.

[41]
POSITIONS

One of the most important aspects of joining a sports team as a young athlete is being assigned a position on a team. Learning your role and the responsibilities required for that position will make you an integral part of the team, as well as challenge you to perform at your personal best. Some athletes may not realize the benefits of understanding how other positions on their team are played, but this knowledge can make your sports experience more rewarding and interesting.

Most team sports feature several positions for players. Sometimes, many athletes are assigned into roles based on offense and defense, whereas other sports may only require a few players to fill positions at a time. As you become familiar with your sport, you can benefit from learning the roles and responsibilities of the different positions involved. This will enhance your understanding and enjoyment of the sport overall and give you insight into what skills are required of your teammates. In addition, grasping the different positions within your sport may give you the opportunity to play a different role someday or even become a substitute if needed.

Ultimately, one of the most important aspects of being a team player is to take responsibility for the role of your athletic position and allow your teammates to do the same for theirs. Even if you understand how to play a different position, it's essential not to criticize how someone else performs it. If you're asked, then you can offer constructive criticism or feedback. Until then, be sure to take accountability for your assigned role and give it your best while supporting your teammates in their respective positions.

[42]
PRE-GAME
ROUTINES

Routines are important for athletes at all levels of play. They provide consistent and effective preparation, especially before a competition. Just as it's important to do physical warm-ups before an athletic event, it's essential to develop a pre-game routine so that you're in the proper mindset for the concentration and focus it takes to play your sport.

Your pre-game routine doesn't have to be complicated or time consuming. Ultimately, your goal should be to apply strategic behaviors that cue your mind to prepare for the upcoming game. One example of a pre-game routine might be to gather and check your equipment, put on your uniform, drink some water, and arrive in plenty of time to avoid feeling rushed. Repeating these steps before each game is the key to remaining focused without worrying that you've forgotten to do something. Mindfulness, too, can be an effective part of your pre-game routine. This can include deep breathing exercises, visualization techniques, and even some simple yoga to stay focused and grounded in the present moment.

There are many benefits to practicing mindfulness as part of your pre-game routine, such as reduced anxiety and stress, improved concentration, and flexibility in thinking. Even a brief moment of silent reflection will give you the chance to stabilize your thoughts and emotions while you connect with the environment around you. All these benefits will work to improve your athletic performance as well as your overall mental health.

[43]
POST-GAME
ROUTINES

It may surprise you to learn that having a consistent post-game routine is also an important part of participating in sports. However, allowing your mind to reflect and unwind after competitions is important, just as a cool-down regimen allows your body to relax and recover from athletic activity. Games are often intense, and implementing a post-game routine ensures that you don't fixate on negative thoughts.

Just as your pre-game routine doesn't require a lot of time or steps, your post-game routine should be brief and simple. Again, repetition of the behaviors involved is key to giving your mind space to process the event in a healthy manner before shifting your focus back to other priorities. One example of a post-game routine might include eating a nutritious snack, drinking plenty of water, cleaning your equipment, taking a shower, and relaxing for a few minutes.

Incorporating mindfulness is also a great strategy for a post-game routine. Doing even one or two mindfulness exercises will encourage your brain to transition from "athletic" to "non-athletic" mode. This can help you avoid mental strain and potential burnout from focusing too much on sports.

Some people may consider going over the events of a game—good or bad—right after it's over. This can help you assess what went right and what can be improved. However, it's far healthier to give your mind a true break after athletic competition, leaving analysis of the game for another time.

[44]
MAINTENANCE

Nearly all sports require equipment, whether it's for individual or team use. Sports equipment is often expensive, and these items are considered an investment. Having equipment that's in good condition enhances your performance and protects against injury. Therefore, it's important to take care of all your equipment so that it will last as long as possible and maintain its condition and effectiveness.

Some of the equipment you use during practice and games may belong to your coaches, the team community, or your school. Many of these items are likely to be costly and would be expensive to replace if lost or damaged. In that case, it's especially important to take care of shared equipment to give you and others the chance to use it in good, clean condition. Doing your part reflects good sportsmanship and respect for your team as a whole.

In terms of your personal sports equipment, maintaining it keeps it functioning properly so that it can be used from season to season. This not only reflects the pride and respect you have for yourself as an athlete but also the investment made by those who purchased the items.

The better care you take of your equipment, the better it serves your athletic performance, and the more protection it provides to prevent injury. This is especially true when it comes to helmets, guards, pads, and other protective gear. Keeping these items clean and in good shape is important for your performance and protection.

[45]
FAMILY
SUPPORT

It may be surprising to see how much support your families provide when it comes to your sporting events. Your biggest fans might include parents and guardians, siblings, and even extended family members. Whether it's providing transportation to practices and competitions, keeping up with your schedule for the season, or cheering you on as spectators, it's important to recognize and express gratitude for your family's support of you as an athlete.

Sometimes, their support is shown in obvious ways such as attending games, helping you maintain your uniform and/or equipment, or providing healthy team snacks. However, your family probably supports your athletics in less noticeable ways as well, such as showing interest in your personal goals and being there for you emotionally during both wins and losses.

One thoughtful way to acknowledge and show appreciation for your family's support is to take a moment and directly thank them—individually or as a group. Even if you aren't sure of how to fully express your gratitude with words, saying thank you or even writing a thank-you note can go a long way.

In addition, you can show how much you value your family's support by offering to help with household chores, such as cooking, cleaning, laundry, and lawn maintenance. Your words and actions will reflect your appreciation of your family's support and the overall gratitude you feel toward them.

[46]
CRITICISM AND
FEEDBACK

The word *criticism* often has negative connotations, as most people associate it with judgment and disapproval. Constructive criticism, however, is intended as specific feedback to help someone improve. For example, telling a player that they "look asleep" on the field isn't exactly helpful and just feels mean; a more constructive way to give feedback to this player might be, "Make sure to move around a bit in the outfield to keep your muscles warm and your mind alert."

Providing constructive criticism is a huge part of a coach or trainer's job in sports. In fact, anyone with expertise in an athletic skill or activity—such as assistants or experienced teammates—may provide constructive criticism to players for more successful outcomes.

In general, if constructive criticism is delivered effectively, people usually receive it in a positive manner. This is especially true if the feedback is clear and gives advice about how to improve. After all, the people involved in your sport likely have the same goals of a successful and positive experience for everyone. Giving feedback involves providing instruction and reinforcement so that everyone can continue to improve their skills and gain a deeper understanding of your sport.

Understandably, it can be difficult when someone corrects you or suggests doing something in a different way. However, if you remember that constructive criticism comes from a place of expertise, care, and consideration, it's much easier to accept it in a positive way.   Another thing to keep in mind when handling criticism is that action in sports usually happens at a fast pace with high emotions. This may not give your coaches and teammates time to adequately prepare or think about what they want to say beforehand. This doesn't excuse harsh or unfair statements, of course, but it can help you remember that you shouldn't take criticism personally. If you feel uncertain about the feedback you've received, consider talking to your coach during a calm moment to get clarification.

[47]
CURRENT EVENTS

Although it may seem like individual sports stay relatively the same, many are changing over time. These developments can include updated rules and regulations, enhanced safety measures and equipment, and even shifts in eligibility for play. When you keep up with what's going on in your sport, you'll have the most up-to-date information to make decisions.

Many young athletes follow professional teams that play the same sport. This is an excellent way to keep up with new developments, especially in terms of statistics, higher-level skills, ways to limit the risk of injury, and rule changes. For example, the National Football League (NFL) adjusted its approach to kick returns as a means of reducing concussions for the 2024 season.

Even though many policies overlap, professional sports are often played much differently than youth sports. Because of this, another good strategy for staying informed about developments in your sport is to pay close attention to what your coaches and trainers say during team meetings and practices.

Keeping up with developments in your sport can also provide opportunities for you to create closer ties with your community. Many athletic organizations sponsor volunteer or fundraising events for the people in their area. For example, you may learn that there is a local sports clinic for new players or disabled athletes, which would give you a chance to share your athletic skills while participating in something personally rewarding. You may also find that fellow team members and their families have organized a donation drive for things like food, toys, and clothing, which can offer you the chance to contribute to your community and support other people involved in your sport.

[48]
PERSONAL
LIMITS

Everyone has limits, from the newest and youngest of athletes to the most experienced professionals. It's important to recognize and be aware of your physical and mental limits to avoid injury, strain, and stress, which can lead to health problems and burnout. When you play within your limits, you'll optimize your competitive skills and be able to fully enjoy your sport.

Most people are at least somewhat aware of their physical limits. In general, athletes train to overcome certain limitations by improving their speed, agility, and endurance. However, your body can only perform to the best of its *individual* ability. Understanding this will keep you from overtraining or attempting risky athletic behaviors that could lead to injury.

For example, for a softball pitcher, it's essential to recognize the limits of your pitching arm, especially if it's a "windmill" pitch. Overusing your arm through excessive practice or gameplay will *not* enhance or improve your pitching performance. Instead, pushing beyond your physical limits — or not taking time to rest and recover after normal activity — could leave you at risk for muscle, joint, and tissue injuries. Severe injuries could potentially end your ability to participate in softball or other sports altogether.

Although your body is likely to warn you when you're pushing your physical limits, it may be more difficult to recognize pain and fatigue when you're pushing your mental boundaries as well. Most sports take as much mental strength as they do physical exertion in terms of learning, concentration, and adapting. Just like your body, your mind is at risk if you push yourself too hard without adequate breaks. Overworking your brain could result in negative self-talk, difficulty balancing athletics with other priorities, team conflict, and worrying too much about competitions.

If you find that you're experiencing mental stress beyond your limit, talk about it with a trusted adult such as a coach, parent, or guardian. These people can help you adjust and find the resources you need to mentally reset.

[49]
CHALLENGES

Like most things in life, playing a sport is full of challenges. In this case, a challenge is a problem or difficulty that requires a solution to overcome. For example, you might find it a challenge to manage your time between sports and other activities, or you might feel challenged when learning a new athletic skill, adjusting to a new position, or resolving a conflict with a teammate.

In the moment, challenges can produce negative reactions; however, they often provide opportunities for growth when you embrace them. Part of embracing challenges as a young athlete is maintaining a healthy perspective. This can take time and effort to develop, but it will help you learn to welcome challenges in all areas of your life, both now and in the future.

Keeping a healthy perspective involves avoiding negative self-talk and expectations of perfection. It's essential to be realistic in your approach to athletics. Remember that everyone makes mistakes and needs time to learn! The more positive and encouraging you are toward yourself on your journey, the easier it'll be to grow and cope with challenges.

It can be difficult to avoid feeling frustrated, stressed, and even overwhelmed as a young athlete. If you notice that you're struggling to find a balance, or if you feel discouraged or stuck, consider talking to someone you trust. This could be your coach, trainer, teammate, or a family member. They'll likely understand the way you're feeling, and they can provide assistance or support to help ease the pressure. Expressing your thoughts and emotions is a healthy way to embrace challenges. It also gives you the opportunity to grow, learn from your experiences, build personal strength, and connect with others.

[50]
LEADERSHIP
SKILLS

One of the benefits of participating in sports as a young athlete is the opportunity to learn and develop leadership skills. This not only makes you a valuable team player, but it will also ensure your future success in other areas such as college or your first job.

All leaders have certain qualities that make them effective; they're generally confident, respectful, and knowledgeable. In addition, good leaders demonstrate clear communication, decision-making, and listening skills while taking responsibility for their decisions.

It takes time and experience to develop leadership qualities. One way you can cultivate these traits, both personally and within your team, is to actively listen to and communicate with others. Sharing ideas not only fosters respect and better relationships among teammates, but it also encourages people to feel connected and think creatively for the benefit of the group. In addition, it's important to respect and learn from your coaches, trainers, and other officials.

Keep in mind that you don't have to be a team captain or hold an official leadership position to develop these skills. You can also do so by improving your knowledge about your sport, connecting with your teammates, and being accountable for your actions. This will build your confidence and present opportunities for others to notice your growth and strengths.

As a leader, it's important to be open and responsive to feedback from others. As you cultivate leadership qualities within yourself and your team, you'll have the confidence to take initiative and become a leader in sports and other areas of your life as well.

[51]
TACTICS

Successfully playing a sport requires an understanding of its related tactics, which are specific actions taken to reach a goal. In sports, tactics include the strategies you use to score points, defend your goal, or outwit the other team. Of course, athletic skills and abilities are a big part of winning in your sport, but you should learn the strategic aspects to enhance how your team performs together.

For example, basketball players practice shooting, dribbling, jumping, and passing; however, just mastering these skills won't necessarily make them good or successful players. Understanding how to use these skills together in a strategy is just as important as being able to perform them in competition. Timing, for instance, is an essential tactic for effective shooting. Communication among teammates is necessary for successful passing, and awareness of the ball and its position can facilitate rebounds and scoring. This combination of athletic skills and tactics is the foundation for most sports.

Grasping the strategic aspects of your sport, no matter what you play, will make participation more enjoyable too. Creating tactical strategies and implementing them during competition can be a rewarding part of teamwork and make your sport more interesting.

[52]
CONFIDENCE

As a young athlete, the journey to gaining confidence in playing your sport can feel long and tiring. You may notice teammates or opponents who seem to play with ease and self-assurance and wonder if you'll ever reach that point. Thankfully, there are strategic ways to nurture and build your athletic confidence along with your overall success.

One of the best ways to build confidence is through time and experience. In sports, this involves dedicating yourself to practicing, training, and developing your skills. The more you participate in a sport, the more you'll learn. For example, if you're a golfer, it may be challenging at first to coordinate your swing and hit the ball accurately toward the hole. However, with practice and concentration, your movements will become more fluid and precise, leading to greater confidence in your abilities.

In this case, it's also important to resist comparing yourself to others, as that can undermine your own confidence. Instead, measure your progress and growth while celebrating all the ways in which you've improved.

Another way to nurture your confidence and future success is to practice believing in yourself. This doesn't mean inflating your abilities or assuming that you're better than others. Instead, it's about developing the self-assurance to know that you can persevere and overcome obstacles. Consider taking regular moments for self-reflection and remembering positive outcomes in which you demonstrated your ability to adapt, grow, and prevail.

[53]
PERSONAL
IMPROVEMENT

Most people would agree that the very foundation of sports is competition. After all, that's what draws people to athletic events, as both players and spectators, with the understanding that the "best" team or competitor will be the winner. However, placing all your focus on beating your opponent takes away from another key principle of sports: striving for your personal best.

Athletes are typically driven and self-disciplined. Winning games, tournaments, and championships is an important part of measuring success, but it's not the only way to win, especially when it comes to your individual accomplishments. In addition to team statistics of wins and losses, many athletes measure and keep track of their personal achievements. These include examples such as batting average, individual points scored, and passing or running yardage.

Keeping track of personal statistics allows you to focus on their individual goals, which, in turn, benefit their teams. For young athletes, measuring your personal development takes the strength and endurance you have built into account. You should also consider the time and energy you've contributed to your team's overall success.

Striving for personal improvement rather than competitive wins enhances your athletic performance and helps maintain your morale, no matter how many victories or defeats you experience. Your personal stats will help you determine how effective your practicing, training, and skill-building techniques have proven. They also provide you with a sense of individual achievement without diminishing any team victories earned in competitions.

[54]
SMALL WINS

So much of sports is focused on winning, whether it's single games, competitions, playoffs, or championships. This emphasis on competitive wins can overshadow many of the successes and achievements that don't result in official acknowledgment. In fact, small victories take place regularly, and they should be acknowledged and celebrated just as much as the big ones.

There are many ways for players to achieve a big win in sports, such as scoring a goal, hitting a home run, making a touchdown, shooting a three-pointer, and coming in first in a race. These actions should all be celebrated and remembered, of course, as should game and season victories. However, it's also important for you to recognize and appreciate the smaller victories as well. These may include making a key play, assisting a teammate with a pass, achieving a personal best, and even showing significant improvement in an athletic skill.

Even if nobody else seems to notice or remember, it's perfectly fine for you to acknowledge and celebrate small wins by yourself. Take the time to congratulate others for their personal athletic achievements as well.

In a sense, taking part in a sport is an achievement in its own right. You should be proud of yourself for the initiative, effort, and commitment it takes to play a sport, even if it's just for one season. Not everyone will be a "star" player, but you can be an important part of a team through your enthusiasm, dedication, and sportsmanship. These small wins add up over time, enhancing your confidence and providing you with important lessons for the future.

[55]
TEAM
TRADITIONS

One of the most meaningful aspects of participating in a sport is its associated traditions. Many of these are unique, and they often encourage social and cultural connections. For example, if you're a fan of professional hockey, you know that the championship team each year is awarded the Stanley Cup. Baseball fans are likely familiar with the traditional seventh inning stretch and singing "Take Me Out to the Ball Game." Even competitions embrace certain traditions such as hosting a special opening ceremony at the Olympics.

As a young athlete, your team may not have the same traditions as those in the professional leagues, but you probably have customs that've been handed down over the years. Many athletic events play the national anthem before competitions or conduct a formal coin toss on the field.

Your specific team might have a certain cheer or routine that brings everyone together before each game. In addition, many teams hold annual banquets to recognize players and coaches with awards. Your individual team may also wrap up the end of the season with a pizza party or another celebration.

Part of good sportsmanship and being a valuable team player is respecting and embracing the traditions associated with your sport. Whether you're a member of a championship team or not, participating in traditions will give you a sense of pride and belonging, in addition to establishing stronger relationships with your teammates. These rituals will also create meaningful memories for you to look back on in the future.

[56]
WEATHER CONDITIONS

Since most outdoor sports are played over a set number of weeks during the year, players are likely to face a variety of weather conditions. These can include rainy and snowy days in addition to sunny ones. You may even enjoy occasionally playing in light rain or snow.

Since some sports are played no matter the weather unless the conditions are extreme, it's important for you to prepare for bad weather and adapt your strategies to avoid injury or illness. This means wearing proper gear that's in good condition and taking precautions if the area becomes wet or slippery.

It may be surprising to know how much the temperature can affect young athletes. This is especially true when the weather is hot and humid. Children don't sweat as much as adults, so it takes longer to adapt to high temperatures.

Because of this, hot conditions can result in serious consequences such as cramps, heat exhaustion, and even heat stroke. To avoid these conditions, you should stay hydrated, take frequent breaks to cool down, and voice any concerns or physical symptoms immediately. Cold temperatures can also present risks for illness and injury among athletes.

Therefore, it's important to protect against wind chill, skin exposure, and dehydration. Trainers, coaches, and other sports officials should be responsible for keeping you safe during all weather conditions. However, they may not notice when an individual player is struggling to adapt to the weather or temperature. You still need to prepare yourself for what to expect as the weather changes and learn to protect yourself against illness and injury. Don't hesitate to report any signs of physical distress immediately when it comes to yourself and your fellow players.

[57]
BODY LANGUAGE

It might surprise you to learn that most of our communication is conveyed and received through body language. Body language includes physical gestures and facial expressions. For example, you can probably tell if someone is sad just by the way their shoulders and head may droop. Similarly, if you're trying to let someone know that you're joking without saying it, you might wink at them, which is also a form of body language.

Most people are unaware of their body language because it's instinctual and doesn't require the same thought process as communicating through speech. Therefore, we often project both negative and positive body language depending on how we feel.

When it comes to sports, it's important to be aware of negative body language, as it can be viewed as disrespectful or unsportsmanlike. This means preventing yourself from expressing frustration, anger, or disappointment through gestures such as kicking, hitting, or throwing something. Even something as simple as a "dirty look" or rolling your eyes is inappropriately negative in sports and should be avoided.

Instead, young athletes should project positive body language as much as possible. This includes good posture, eye contact, and open facial expressions. Positive body language reflects self-control, respect for others, and overall good sportsmanship. This will not only enhance others' perception of you as a reasonable and confident person, but it will also motivate people to trust and connect with you.

[58]
INJURIES
AND SAFETY

Although it may seem like bad luck or a waste of time to think about sports injuries as a young athlete, the reality is that you're at risk simply by participating. Some injuries such as scrapes, bumps, and small bruises are minor and heal quickly. However, other sports injuries such as head trauma, broken bones, and torn ligaments are serious. Therefore, it's essential to be prepared by learning about common athletic injuries and how to prevent them.

There are many types of potential injuries associated with each sport. Some may be due to contact with other players, such as in football or hockey, and others may be the result of repeated movement, such as in golf or tennis. In youth sports, precautions are taken to protect young athletes from injury as much as possible. However, participants and their parents or guardians should still understand the risks of getting hurt when playing.

Your parents, guardians, coaches, and trainers should emphasize that safety comes first. Players should report any pain, discomfort, or signs of injury immediately. Young athletes shouldn't be encouraged to "play through" or ignore any pain, as this can result in the injury getting worse.

Some basic preventive measures to avoid athletic injury are to properly wear clean protective gear that's in good condition, follow the rules of play, train and practice responsibly, and prioritize self-care. To stay fully informed about how to safely play your sport, talk with your family doctor, sports coach, or athletic trainer.

[59]
TRAINING
PLANS

Not all youth sports programs offer training plans for athletes. However, players can benefit from training schedules when they're made by coaches or athletic trainers. Training plans can help you reach your optimal level of performance by practicing key techniques, learning new skills, and getting stronger over time.

Following your training plan allows you to steadily improve your skills while building strength, endurance, and resilience. A consistent training regimen can also help with time management and maintaining a balance between your commitment to sports and other activities. This includes scheduling days off for your body and mind to rest and recover.

Another advantage of sticking to a consistent training plan, especially for young athletes, is that it reduces the risk of injury. Your training plan should be designed to fit your athletic skills and abilities, in addition to your age and physical development. This provides a balance between strengthening your progress and protecting you from overtraining.

[60]
BURNOUT

Burnout is a feeling of physical, mental, and emotional exhaustion that stems from trying to do too much without a break. All types of people experience burnout. It can be the result of a too much pressure, limited time for relaxation, lack of support, and overworking. To avoid any lasting effects, young athletes — along with their families, coaches, and trainers — should know how to recognize the signs of burnout so that it can be immediately addressed.

You may feel unmotivated or uninterested when you're experiencing burnout. Some physical signs may include loss of appetite, difficulty sleeping, nausea, and unusual aches or pains. Mental symptoms of burnout can include anxiety, nervousness, irritability, trouble focusing, and fatigue. There's a significant difference between feeling tired from playing sports and being completely worn out. That's why it's essential to be aware of the signs of burnout so that you can take a break to recover.

Some people may believe that pushing through and continuing to play will overcome burnout. However, this approach is likely to create more damage and larger issues in the future, especially for young athletes. The best strategy is to take a complete break from all training and competition in your sport for a set amount of time, without any guilt or regret. You should also talk to your doctor to rule out illness or injury and seek supportive counseling if necessary.

As you regain your mental and physical health, you and the responsible adults in your life can determine the best way to return to your sport. Until then, the focus should be on your rest and recovery.

[61]
CROSS-TRAINING
BENEFITS

Cross-training is an athletic approach that incorporates styles of training for players to improve their performance as a whole. This usually involves a combination of various exercises and training methods, including techniques from other sports. Cross-training builds different muscles and can make practices more enjoyable by adding new activities.

You've probably developed a specific set of skills and athletic abilities related to your sport. However, training for just one sport may limit your overall strength, stamina, agility, and speed. Cross-training counteracts this by incorporating exercises that target other muscle groups and build different athletic skills.

For example, cross-country runners use certain muscle groups, breathing techniques, and other aerobic strategies to maintain consistent speed and endurance. In this case, participating in a cross-training program that focuses on low-impact exercise like swimming, cycling, or yoga can be beneficial for recovery and to prevent overexertion.

Ultimately, cross-training provides you with more balanced training regimen for your entire body. It can also improve your overall health and well-being. In addition, participating in other athletic activities can generate a sense of new interest and fun. It may even inspire you to try another sport in the future.

[62]
NETWORKING

As a young athlete, playing a sport gives you an excellent chance to meet many different people. This includes not just your teammates but also other athletes, coaches, trainers, and professionals who are involved in your sport. At first, it may seem challenging to make connections with so many individuals, but there are many benefits to these relationships.

One way to build a network of fellow athletes and professionals in your sport is to be open, genuine, and friendly. A positive attitude draws others in, helping you form friendships with other players. Being responsible, sportsmanlike, and enthusiastic will help you stand out to coaches and officials and encourage them to remember you positively in the future.

Perhaps the best way to connect with others in your sport is to show a sincere interest in who they are and express appreciation for their commitment and efforts. However, keep in mind that you must be authentic and honest to form real connections.

Another benefit of connecting with others in your sport is the opportunity to form plans and relationships for the future. For example, you may decide that you'd like to continue playing your sport when you go to college. Having a network of coaches, trainers, and other athletes will help when you have questions, need advice, or require references. They may have their own networks of people who could support your application, help with the scholarship process, or even introduce you for a potential interview.

Ultimately, having a network of people who share your passion for playing a sport is a great way to stay connected, create memories, and maintain friendships. This network can also provide you with opportunities for the future, making it a solid long-term investment.

[63]
TEAM SUCCESS

Playing a team sport is an opportunity for young athletes to learn how to contribute as an individual to the success of a group. Team sports are made up of many positions and roles, all of which do their part in working together to achieve wins. Therefore, it's important to celebrate victories as a team, in addition to individual successes.

When you celebrate as a team, you're acknowledging everyone's contribution. This includes *all* teammates, from star players to those who cheer and show support from the sidelines. Making sure that each player is recognized and appreciated enhances team unity, which improves the team's overall performance. It also emphasizes that everyone is working toward the same goal, which creates a strong sense of community among players.

One way for young athletes to enjoy victories as a team is to include all members. Of course, it's good to celebrate individual successes and achievements, but this shouldn't be at the expense of the team as a whole. Learning how to incorporate all team members in celebrating victories will benefit you in the future, especially in family and social settings, higher education, and your career.

[64]
ADAPTING
TO CHANGES

Change can be difficult to accept, no matter where or when it happens. For example, you may feel confident in your coach because you've been on their team for a while. Similarly, you probably feel comfortable with your teammates because they're friends in addition to being fellow athletes. Unfortunately, coaches sometimes transfer to a different team or even leave the sport altogether, and the same can be true for teammates. That's why it's essential to learn how to embrace change so that you can adapt to whatever comes your way.

One reason that sports can play such a big role in people's lives is the emotional attachment it brings. When something changes, you not only need to adapt to the new situation but also the emotional shift involved in welcoming something different. The key is to give yourself time to adjust while keeping a positive mental attitude.

You may find that a new coach or player is an asset to your team even if their approach is different. They may implement a change in strategy that benefits you, and they may even become a mentor or close friend.

Keep in mind that the wonderful memories of each sports season and the people involved will always be with you. However, adapting to changing people, strategies, and situations creates room for growth, new experiences, and potential friendships. Adaptation is an essential skill in all areas of life, so learning this ability will benefit you in other ways as well.

[65]
TECHNOLOGY

The role of technology has grown in the world of sports even at the youth level. The tools and resources designed to enhance athletic training and performance can be helpful when used properly.

Young athletes may find online tutorials and even virtual training programs to be good resources for learning and improving certain skills. This is especially true for players with different learning styles who may need supplemental materials beyond practice and training in person. Analytics programs may also be helpful in providing feedback and statistics to measure your areas of improvement and overall performance. Even communicating through social media can be useful to connect with teammates and other people who are interested in your sport.

Although there are many positive aspects of using technology for training and analysis in your sport, it's vital to do so wisely and responsibly. For example, too much screen time—especially on social media—can be counterproductive to your athletic development and mental well-being. In addition, not every tutorial will give accurate or healthy advice, and focusing too much on stats and numbers can interfere with your natural ability and pure enjoyment of your sport. Therefore, it's important to limit your use of technology so that it doesn't undermine your real-life experience as an athlete.

[66]
FEEDBACK

Feedback, like constructive criticism, can be helpful to young athletes. Feedback from coaches, trainers, and experienced players can teach you more about your personal skills, performance, and areas for improvement. Always be open to the suggestions, informed opinions, and observations of those with expertise in your sport who have your best interests at heart.

Most feedback in sports comes from coaches. They provide feedback to individual players and the team as a whole. Your goal is to be open to what they say and do your best to try their suggestions. Don't be afraid to ask for clarification if you receive feedback that you don't quite understand. Good coaches realize that not every athlete learns at the same rate or in the same manner, and they should encourage you to ask questions and discuss their feedback.

Although it may seem intimidating at first, sometimes it's good to be proactive in seeking out feedback rather than waiting for someone to provide it. For example, when your coach has time, you can ask for their opinion about your performance. It's best to be specific and direct with your questions in these cases. Instead of just asking how well you're playing, you should ask your coach for feedback about your batting stance, running form, or other measurable skill. In return, be appreciative in your response and open to implementing any suggestions for improvement.

[67]
FAN DYNAMICS

Sports fans are among the most loyal and fun-loving people. In general, they appreciate all aspects of the game and offer support to players and teams. When it comes to youth sports, fans are most likely made up of players' friends and family, along with members of the community who enjoy attending games and competitions.

At first, it may feel awkward or intimidating to play in front of people you don't know. However, it's important to remember that fans often have a positive effect in sports just by showing up to cheer for the teams and players they favor. Knowing people are rooting for you can reinforce your confidence and enhance the joy and excitement of playing. Fans may also contribute to sports organizations through volunteering their time or supporting fundraising programs.

Unfortunately, there may be times when certain fans get caught up in the emotions of competition and behave in impolite or inappropriate ways such as using foul language or gestures. You can navigate this type of fan dynamic by respectfully ignoring them or reporting it to a coach or another athletic official. In general, most fans contribute positively to the experience, and it's best not to engage with those who are exceptions to the rule.

[68]
PRE-GAME
PLAYLISTS

Music can have a positive influence on athletic performance by impacting how you think and feel before a game. Listening to music can reduce stress, improve focus, uplift mood, and decrease fatigue. For young athletes, creating a playlist as part of a pre-game routine is an effective way to pump up energy and have fun before games.

Music can have significant effects on the way we feel physically, emotionally, and mentally. For example, music with a faster tempo can actually stimulate the heart rate and circulatory system to help with an athlete's speed and endurance. Positive lyrics can also stimulate the brain to increase feelings of self-confidence and optimism before competition.

For your pre-game playlist, it's important to choose upbeat music with songs that inspire and motivate you. You can find example playlist for athletes online if you need suggestions to get you started. Keep in mind that you don't have to listen to every song, and you can shuffle your selections depending on what appeals to you before each competition.

[69]
YOGA FOR ATHLETES

Yoga is becoming more widespread than ever as people of all ages and backgrounds realize the enormous health benefits it has to offer. Yoga is especially helpful for athletes since as encourages you to be mentally present and aware of your body. You can incorporate yoga sessions into your daily life and training regimen to improve things like flexibility, mental focus, strength, and balance.

Yoga is a calming activity designed to build connections between the mind and body. Practicing yoga involves specific poses and positions, exercises for breathing, and routines that promote mindfulness through meditation. It's important to practice properly to get the most benefits from yoga and avoid injury. You can look for yoga classes at local community centers or through reputable tutorials online. Be sure to check in with your coach and your doctor before beginning a yoga regimen to make sure it's safe for you to start.

In addition to physical benefits, yoga is also great for mindfulness and improving mental focus. The combination of meditation and regulated breathing in yoga allows athletes to relax their thoughts and strengthen their concentration, reducing stress and enhancing overall athletic performance. Yoga also provides an opportunity for visualization and developing a positive mindset. Players who commit to doing yoga regularly, in both the on and off seasons, will enjoy the rewards of greater physical and mental well-being.

[70]
GRATITUDE

You may not realize it, but the ability and opportunity to play a sport is a privilege in many ways. There are several factors which can make it difficult or impossible for young people to participate in athletics, whether due to physical, economic, or social limitations. Understanding your good fortune in being able to play your sport is a wonderful chance to practice gratitude.

Gratitude is a feeling of appreciation for the good things in your life. Practicing gratitude means reflecting on these advantages and expressing thanks, whether internally or out loud. In many ways, the practice of gratitude is as much about recognizing your fortunate circumstances as it is about directly expressing your thanks. Feeling such appreciation often leads to greater empathy, kindness, and generosity, which can allow you to give back to others and treat them with compassion.

Of course, practicing gratitude can also remind you to thank those who support you as a young athlete, such as your family members, coaches, and community. Ultimately, cultivating gratitude for all your opportunities is a wonderful character trait that will remind you of the good things in your life.

[71]
PROGRESS
AND GOALS

As a young athlete, you may be interested in recording your progress and successes in playing your sport. One way to do this is by keeping a journal. You can use a notebook, computer, or even your phone to log your personal stats, athletic goals, and general reflections. This will allow you to track your growth within your sport as well as in other areas of life.

Keeping a journal to track your growth in sports allows you to document your achievements and see how far you've come as a player. Taking time to reflect and write down your thoughts may give you clarity about long-term goals you wish to achieve or activities that don't interest you anymore.

For example, you may have started practicing and competing in gymnastics at a young age because your parent or guardian thought you would enjoy it. Now that you're older, you just don't like it as much as you used to in the past. Recording your thoughts in a journal may help you realize that you want to move on to a different sport or activity.

Some people find it stressful to keep a journal because it's another thing to think about every day. However, your journal is strictly for your own benefit and meant to be read only by you. If you're too tired to write every day, then aim for a couple times a week. Your writing doesn't need to be perfect.

The goal is for you to have a record of your progress and a deeper understanding of your growth as an athlete and a person. Use your journal as a means of connecting with your thoughts and feelings in addition to keeping track of your stats, improvements, and lessons learned.

[72]
MINDFUL
EATING

Young athletes often work up a big appetite when practicing and playing sports. Hunger and an active metabolism can make lazy eating habits seem harmless. Unfortunately, when people aren't mindful of their eating habits, they often consume empty calories and miss out on the healthy, balanced benefits of nutritious food. If this becomes a regular habit, it can ultimately affect your performance and overall well-being.

Most people have some experience with mindless eating, such as snacking on a bag of potato chips while watching TV. Eating while distracted can keep you from recognizing when you feel full, leading to overeating and oversized portions of nutritionally inadequate foods. Mindful eating, on the other hand, is being aware of what you are consuming and how much.

For example, eating dinner with your family when everyone is focused on their food and present in the moment encourages mindful eating. It's much easier to choose healthy options with better nutrition when you pay attention to what you're eating. This is why most people don't snack on salads at the movies or eat a full bag of potato chips during a family meal.

Of course, young athletes aren't expected to always eat perfectly nutritious food in exactly the right-sized portions. It's probably fine to indulge in pizza, fast food, and even processed snacks once in a while, especially if you and your teammates are celebrating after a game or traveling to a competition. However, it's best to eat mindfully and choose healthy, nutritious foods whenever possible so that your body can function at its best.

[73]
COMPARISONS

There's an old saying that "comparison is the thief of joy." That means that comparing yourself to others can make you feel bad about your own progress and achievements. Therefore, it's important to focus on your own journey and avoid measuring how you stack up against others.

In many ways, comparisons are unfair because you're looking at someone from *your* perspective, which doesn't present the whole picture or all the relevant information, especially on social media. For example, if you're a swimmer and you compare yourself to a top competitor, you're more likely to undervalue your own performance because you're only seeing their successes. They aren't going online to post about their failures or mistakes. The next time you're tempted to compare yourself to someone else, remember that you're only seeing the highlights they want to show other people.

It can be difficult to avoid comparisons, especially within the sport you play. That's why you should stop when you find yourself making comparisons and focus on your own athletic journey instead. This can include reflecting on your athletic achievements, the effort you've put in, and all that you've learned. By concentrating on your experiences rather than making assumptions about other athletes, you'll develop a more positive viewpoint and a fairer perspective.

[74]
LEARNING
FROM LOSSES

There are many experiences in sports that young athletes can learn from, and defeat is one of them. Even though nobody enjoys losing, it can provide an opportunity to learn and improve in the future. Focusing on learning a lesson from defeat can also help you find meaning in the experience and overcome negative feelings.

Treat mistakes that result in defeat as learning opportunities. For example, if you make an error on the field or do something that results in a penalty, you can examine what happened and avoid the same mistake in the future. Another lesson might come from recognizing a breakdown in communication between you and your teammates, which can encourage you to work on improving your communication skills for the rest of the season. Learning to extract lessons from losses will enhance your athletic performance and value as a team member.

Although you can learn from defeat in sports, it's unhealthy to dwell on negative thoughts. This includes putting yourself down or obsessively analyzing what went wrong. Losing is as much a part of being an athlete as winning, and sometimes the outcome in sports is a negative one through nobody's fault. If there are obvious lessons to be learned from a loss, then it's fine to acknowledge, learn from, and internalize them. However, it's also healthy to learn to put defeats behind you and move on to the next step.

[75]
RISK-TAKING
IN GAMES

One of the most exciting aspects of sports is the strategy involved in playing each game. Some strategies may be riskier than others, such as attempting to steal a base in softball or taking a three-point shot in basketball. Overall, taking risks during games and competitions can lead to rewards that benefit your team and your personal athletic contribution. However, these risks should be well thought out as much as possible.

A calculated risk is one that's taken thoughtfully with adequate planning behind it. During practice or training, your coach may point out certain chances or opportunities that could come up during a game and encourage players to take the risk if they feel confident in doing so. In other circumstances, you may find an opportunity by paying close attention and decide to take the risk of doing something out of the ordinary. This may include passing to a different player, running an unusual play, or taking an unexpected shot that can work in your favor.

Although there may be a moderate risk-reward balance in your sport, it's essential to avoid high-risk decisions and behaviors during competitions, especially without consulting the rest of your team. Taking a significant athletic risk can come at a high cost that could include injuring yourself or another player. Risky behaviors could also result in errors or penalties that actually benefit your opponents, resulting in an unnecessary loss. That's why it's important to calculate the cost of any risks that you plan to take as a player and communicate with your coach, trainer, and team beforehand.

[76]
COMMUNITY INVOLVEMENT

Sports are an excellent way to get involved in and give back to your community. As a young athlete, you might not have considered the importance of supporting local businesses and worthy causes for neighbors in need. However, finding a way to make a difference in your community is a rewarding experience that you can build on for your future.

Many sports organizations have local sponsors such as businesses and shops that provide funding to help young athletes have equipment, uniforms, safe places to play, and so on. One way to give back to those who support local athletic programs is to frequent their businesses and encourage others to do the same.

For example, if you know that your local pizzeria is an athletic sponsor, consider eating there with your family and friends rather than a national chain restaurant. They will appreciate the business, and you'll feel good about supporting them. You can also find out which local companies contribute to your sport and send them a thank-you note. This is an especially nice gesture if your teammates sign it as well.

Another way to be involved in your community is to participate in local volunteer efforts, whether individually or as a team. This could be anything from cleaning up a local park to visiting local nursing homes. No matter how you get involved in your community as a young athlete, your support and gratitude will create a brighter experience for everyone and, hopefully, encourage you to keep giving back in the future.

[77]
SPORTSMANSHIP
IN DEFEAT

Losing in sports can be a tough thing to handle; in fact, psychologists have found that a negative outcome in a competition actually produces a stronger effect on the brain and body than a positive outcome. To put it simply, athletes don't play to lose, and as a result, they must spend extra energy to overcome the consequences of loss. This can lead to anger, resentment, frustration, and sadness, especially for young athletes who may be new to the experience of defeat.

Since losing is a reality in sports no matter what you play or how athletic you are, it's essential to learn how to cope with defeat and accept losses with grace. In this situation, grace means demonstrating courtesy and goodwill in your behavior after experiencing defeat. It's not easy to accept a loss with grace under most circumstances, but this can be especially challenging if the loss is unexpected. Hopefully, your coaches and more experienced teammates will set a good example, but this is a skill you should also develop for yourself.

Accepting defeat with grace requires you to acknowledge that not everything will go your way all the time. You don't have to feel happy about losing, but you should still show respect for your teammates and opponents regardless of which team won.

[78]
ATHLETIC RIVALRIES

Friendly rivalries that take place between teams or individual players are part of the fun of sports. Fans often participate in this aspect of athletics to show their loyalty to a team, city, college, or player. For example, the rivalry between the New York Yankees and Boston Red Sox is infamous in Major League Baseball, as is the rivalry between the University of North Carolina (UNC) and Duke University in NCAA basketball.

A rivalry simply means that two individuals or teams are in competition for the same thing. In sports, rivals compete for victory in competitive events like games, series, and tournaments. However, sometimes players or sports fans take rivalries too seriously, and this can lead to negative consequences on and off the field.

It's natural and generally in good fun to consider a rival opponent as an adversary within a sportsmanlike frame of mind during a game or competition. However, making a rival team or competitor out to be an enemy or villain is disrespectful and can even be harmful, especially if it results in making mean comments or bullying.

As a young athlete, it's important to understand rivalries so that you know how to treat everyone with respect and sportsmanlike conduct. This means always being courteous toward your opponents, their fans, and sports officials. Even if opposing players or spectators taunt you, it's essential to react with respect and let your coach or other authority figure handle the situation. In addition, you should always remain sportsmanlike during competition and leave the rivalry behind when the game's over.

[79]
STUDYING
AND EDUCATION

Most young athletes really enjoy playing their sport and take it as a serious commitment. This interest and passion can lead to learning and building up a good deal of knowledge about their sport, which is a wonderful thing.

However, unlike professional athletes, you probably attend school for six to eight hours each weekday and have homework assignments and projects to do on your own time. It can be tough to balance the things you *have* to learn and the topics you actually enjoy studying.

It may be surprising to learn how often sports can intersect with academic subjects. For example, many famous players, teams, and competitions are tied to historical events, such as the significant 1919 World Series and the "Black Sox Scandal." This scandal is also featured in one of the most well-known works of American literature: *The Great Gatsby*.

Physics and math are also subjects that directly influence the world of sports, from enhancing modern equipment to compiling and recording all manner of athletic statistics. If you're feeling unmotivated in a particular academic area, finding a connection with your sports knowledge may inspire you to embrace further learning.

Education is important in both the academic and athletic arenas, so it's important to balance your sports knowledge with school subjects. In fact, your achievements in education can lead directly to athletic advantages in high school, college, and your future career. This may include better test scores, scholarships, and admission to competitive universities. Basically, a well-rounded education will contribute to your intelligence and understanding of the world so that you can be successful in all you do.

[80]
SUPPORT SYSTEMS

It can be stressful to navigate school, family, extracurricular activities, and commitments to your sport all at the same time. Thankfully, having a support system can help you stay balanced even under stress. When you open yourself up to people who care, you'll find yourself surrounded by a supportive network of people with your best interests at heart.

There are many people in your life who can be part of your support network. Coaches, trainers, and fellow players are important to include in your support system because they understand your situation and the commitment it takes to play your sport. You can turn to them for advice, encouragement, and understanding. Family members, friends, and counselors are also important to have in your support network. When you want to talk or you feel overwhelmed, make sure to let someone know and give them a chance to find time in their schedule to help.

There's one other important member of your support system: *you*. Just as your supportive network can provide you with guidance, care, and encouragement, you can do your part by prioritizing your health and well-being. This means getting adequate rest and nutrition while also practicing positive thinking and self-talk. Being part of your own support system will help you reduce stress and anxiety, improve your self-confidence, and enhance your athletic performance.

[81]
ELECTROLYTES

Electrolytes are important minerals that help your body function. Some of the main electrolytes your body needs are sodium, potassium, calcium, magnesium, and chloride. They maintain hydration, balance acidity levels, and help regulate your muscle movements and central nervous system. People lose electrolytes through sweating and urination. An imbalance in these minerals can cause symptoms such as headaches, nausea, cramping, fatigue, and reduced energy.

Most people maintain their electrolyte balance and hydration levels by eating nutritious foods and drinking plenty of water. However, athletes who participate in intense exercise that lasts for over an hour and results in heavy sweating may require additional electrolytes. This may also be the case for athletes competing in hot and humid weather conditions since the resulting increase in sweating depletes electrolyte levels in the body.

Although many sports drinks advertise the benefits of electrolytes, they often contain unnecessary sugar and food coloring. Overall, it's better to maintain hydration by drinking unsweetened electrolyte drinks and eating foods rich in vitamins and minerals.

[82]
CROSS-CULTURAL DIVERSITY

Hopefully, as a young athlete, you will benefit from a culturally diverse team. This means that your team is made up of members from different backgrounds who have various beliefs and unique experiences. An inclusive team environment ensures that everyone feels welcomed and appreciated regardless of cultural differences.

Sometimes, it can be challenging to know how to show respect for other people's cultures and beliefs. If you make a mistake and a teammate lets you know that what you did was offensive, make sure you fully understand how to avoid the same situation in the future. Learning and changing your behavior will make your team a more inclusive place for everyone.

Above all, it's essential to avoid making any judgments or forming negative opinions simply because someone speaks, dresses, behaves, or views the world differently than you. As a team member, you have a responsibility to ensure that each player is valued for who they are—no matter their culture or origins. You can achieve this by learning about and understanding each teammate as an individual and embracing the diversity of the team as a whole.

[83]
FUN IN TRAINING

It's normal to view training and practicing as work or a way to build the skills you need to participate in the "real fun" during games and competitions. It's true that workouts and practice can feel repetitive without the payoff of a competitive win; however, finding joy in the process of training makes athletics much more positive and rewarding.

One good way to find a sense of fun during practice is to appreciate the lack of pressure. When you're training, you won't need to deal with spectators or opponents. This allows you to focus on improving your skills and bonding with your teammates. You can also find joy in appreciating personal victories in the training progress, such as improvements in your speed, strength, and endurance.

Finding the fun in practice and training sessions also creates a positive approach to athletics as a whole. This can help you avoid burnout and reinforce your passion for playing your sport. Unlike a single game or athletic competition, advancing your abilities through training and practicing is a process. This means that each skill you earn and stat you improve is a personal victory that demonstrates your hard work and dedication.

[84]
REALISTIC PERSPECTIVES

As you progress in your sport and improve as a player, it's natural to consider your potential future as an athlete. This may include hopes of playing in college or even at the professional or Olympic level. While these are admirable goals, it's also important to be realistic about your athletic career.

There are many stories of athletes who work and train from a young age to become superstars in their sport. These stories are often heartwarming and inspiring. They captivate fans, other athletes, and even casual observers with the exciting narrative of pursuing a dream and working to make it come true.

However, many such sports stories don't directly account for the sheer luck involved in that kind of success. The reality is that only a small percentage of young athletes end up playing at the college level, and even fewer get the chance to go pro or participate in the Olympics. Of course, this doesn't mean you should give up on your athletic dreams. There are benefits to pursuing them, but it's essential to have a variety of other goals to pursue outside of sports as well. You can achieve success without relying solely on athletic dreams.

Whether or not you end up as a college or professional athlete, maintaining a lifelong passion for your sport is a good thing. Many young athletes continue to participate in their sport as adults by playing on community teams, coaching and volunteering, or keeping up with healthy workouts. By forming a realistic perspective for your athletic future, you can nurture a lifetime of interest in sports and continue to build positive experiences and memories.

[85]
FRIENDSHIPS

One of the greatest benefits of playing sports is the opportunity to make new and long-term friends. This is especially true when you're a member of a team. Although you may not form close bonds with all your teammates, and some friendships take longer to build than others, being part of a team provides a strong foundation for companionship through common interests.

It's important to grow and maintain your athletic friendships off the field. Consider inviting one or more of your teammates to hang out on the weekend or during the off season. Get to know them by asking genuine questions that are unrelated to sports, such as their favorite subject in school or what hobbies they enjoy.

Keep in mind that you don't have to limit your friendships to just members of your team. You may find that a player on a different team goes to the same school or lives in the same neighborhood as you. This is an excellent chance to develop a new friendship, especially since you already have a shared interest in common.

Allowing your friendships to grow outside of sports will make them even stronger and more rewarding. You may be surprised at what you have in common outside of athletics, such as a passion for music, video games, or even a completely different sport than the one you play. Exploring mutual interests with your sports friends and teammates also gives you the chance to make lifelong memories and get to know a variety of interesting people. The more you maintain these friendships by staying in touch and nurturing your connections, the more grateful you will feel for the sport you play and the experiences that brought these relationships into your life.

[86]
ATHLETIC OPPONENTS

Schedules for youth sports are almost always created in advance, so you'll likely know the dates and times for competitive events that take place during the season. These schedules usually include the opposing team you will be playing as well, which gives your team a chance to analyze your opponents to identify their strengths and weaknesses. This analysis can give you an advantage when you meet them in competition.

Depending on the level at which you play your sport, your coach may have insights to share or even footage of opposing teams and how they play. This might be discussed during a team meeting so that strategies can be put in place to react to each player on the opposing team.

Of course, it's more important as a young athlete to focus on ways to improve your team's overall performance than it is to study what your opponent is doing. However, information and observations about your competitors can be helpful in some cases.

Always remember that your opponents are not "enemies" by any means, and they still deserve to be treated with respect and good sportsmanship. In fact, there may be a chance in the future that one or more of the players on an opposing team will end up playing on *your* team or vice versa. Because of this, when discussing or analyzing the opposition's strengths and weaknesses, it's essential to behave in a respectful manner without making rude comments. Your fellow athletes deserve courtesy and consideration whether they're on your team or not.

[87]
VOLUNTEER OPPORTUNITIES

One of the best ways to share your passion and interest in sports as a young athlete is to volunteer at sports events. Even making a small contribution to a good cause can be a rewarding experience. This will also give you the chance to develop your sense of empathy and give back to others.

The best place to find opportunities to volunteer at sports events is within your community. You might hear that someone's team needs extra support, or you can ask your parents or guardians to keep an eye out online. For example, your local recreation center may sponsor a 5K run to raise money and need volunteers to help with things handing out water. You may even come across a chance to volunteer for a sports program to help younger or disadvantaged athletes.

Another way to contribute to sports events as a volunteer is to organize a community effort with your teammates or fellow athletes. This may involve a group cleanup of common athletic areas like tennis courts at a local park or a school soccer field. Be sure to get permission from your coach and other officials if necessary. Overall, volunteering your time and energy toward valuable events can be very rewarding, which can motivate further efforts and contributions in the future.

[88]
SCIENTIFIC DISCOVERIES

Sports science is an exciting field, and staying informed about the latest research can enhance your performance, motivation, and overall health as an athlete. Researchers in sports science study everything from injury prevention to nutrition, all with the purpose of improving the lives and experiences of athletes.

There are many websites, podcasts, and videos where you can learn about the latest in sports science research. It's essential, however, to ensure that the information you are taking in comes from reputable sources that are accurate and reliable. The best way to do this is to verify what you've learned with your coach, trainer, doctor, or another knowledgeable adult before you follow any advice. Otherwise, you may put yourself at risk of injury or adopting a habit that actually interferes with your athletic performance.

Sports psychology is one of the largest fields in sports science that has experienced accelerated growth in recent years. Playing any sport requires mental as well as physical effort, and sports psychologists work toward developing methods to support the mental health and well-being of athletes.

This is especially beneficial for young athletes who may not have had the chance to develop adequate coping skills. Even at your age, you're still faced with challenges like the pressure to perform that put you at risk of burnout. Learning about the latest research in sports psychology can help you apply this knowledge to your athletic experience and enhance your mental health and enjoyment of playing at the same time.

[89]
CONTINUOUS IMPROVEMENT

Where setting goals can help young athletes track their progress, it's important to approach them with continuous improvement in mind. If you are playing and practicing consistently, eventually you'll experience losing a game or enduring a period where your performance waivers. This is natural. Successful athletes reframe these moments as an opportunity to improve and re-work their goals.

Whenever you feel bad about your performance, experience a loss, or fail to meet a goal, take a moment to re-work your plan. Focus on the lessons you've learned rather than any regrets. Experienced athletes learn how to transform perceived failure into determination and focus. It's not uncommon for our worst moments to lead to the greatest results.

When setting goals, making the deadline too tight or expecting too much of yourself can sabotage your success. As an athlete, your body requires rest and pushing too hard can lead to injuries. However, not practicing enough will also have a negative effect on your performance. Tracking your goals and the steps you take to reach them is a great tool for identifying what's working and what needs adjustments.

It will take practice to master this skill of continuously course-correcting. Just remember, it's not about perfection, it's about progress. Each perceived failure is an opportunity to fine tune your goals and identify areas for improvement.

[90]
RECOVERY AND
NUTRITION

Most young athletes have a hearty appetite, especially after a game or workout. This is generally a good thing because your body needs to replenish vitamins, minerals, and other nutrients through the food you eat. However, being hungry after athletic activity can also make unhealthy foods, such as fast food and salty or sugary snacks, seem more tempting. Although these choices may be tasty and easily accessible, they won't provide you with effective nutrition for your recovery.

Occasionally, your team may go out to a fast food or pizza restaurant as a group after a game or practice, maybe to celebrate a win or just for fun. In these circumstances, it's understandable to eat less-than-healthy foods. However, to fuel your body with the right nutrients after workouts or competitions, it's important to make healthy choices as often as possible by eating vegetables, fruits, and lean proteins.

Preparing nutritious snacks ahead of time is a great way to avoid eating empty calories. For example, making fruit and veggie slices to have on hand as well as yogurt, a whole wheat peanut butter sandwich, granola, or even a healthy smoothie can give your body essential nutrients for physical recovery and overall health.

In addition to drinking plenty of water, paying careful attention to your nutrition is the key to optimal athletic performance and long-term wellness. A few minutes of planning and preparation for healthy snack options after workouts and games will satisfy your hunger and allow your body to recover properly. Healthy foods also provide a good balance to counteract those times when you do indulge in less nutritious meals.

[91]
HERO
CULTURE

It's common for young athletes to admire professionals who play their sport. This is especially true of pro athletes who get a great deal of attention and notoriety, elevating some of them to "hero" status. Although many professional sports stars are excellent role models as successful players and positive contributors to society, they're still human and often make mistakes that are much more visible to the public than what most "unknown" people experience.

Our culture places a heavy emphasis on sports and physical abilities, sometimes to the exclusion of other positive pursuits and capabilities. In general, a sports scholarship to a college or university is much more comprehensive than an academic one, and a professional athlete's salary is typically far greater than those of a teacher, firefighter, or police officer.

Research shows that a majority of kids in the U.S. consider sports stars to be their heroes. In addition, society often overlooks mistakes and negative behaviors when they're committed by professional athletes. These factors can influence how you see the biggest names in your sport.

It's important to understand that all athletes are human. This means that they make mistakes in spite of being successful in their sports. They should also be held accountable for their actions, no matter how talented or famous they happen to be.

[92]
MENTAL HEALTH
AWARENESS

As a young athlete, your mental health is just as important as your physical health. Although it may not be addressed as often as physical strength in sports, you should be aware of—and prioritize—the strength of your mental health. This means checking in with yourself in terms of how you're coping with potential challenges like stress, burnout, and maintaining a balanced lifestyle. If you notice that you need support, act right away instead of allowing the problem to worsen.

Your mental health directly affects your performance as an athlete. Being able to focus and concentrate is an important skill in every sport. When you're struggling with mental health issues, these skills are compromised, causing you to feel tired, overwhelmed, and discouraged. This can lead to a cycle of decreased self-confidence and self-esteem that negatively affect you even outside of sports. As an athlete and teammate, it is never selfish, weak, or unreasonable to reach out for support when you need it. In fact, it's the right thing to do every time.

Aside from your athletic performance, being aware of and prioritizing your mental health is a lifelong strategy for overall wellness. Just as you would get support for a physical injury or illness, it's essential to seek help any time you feel it's needed for your mental health. Consider the trusted adults in your life, such as family members, coaches, trainers, teachers, and doctors, and let them know when you need such support. Never put off asking for help. The sooner you address difficulties or problems, the sooner they can be treated or resolved. You deserve to feel well in all aspects of your life.

[93]
TRAVEL
ETIQUETTE

Playing sports often involves traveling for away games or competitions. You might take a bus as a group or carpool with coaches, fellow athletes, or family members. No matter how you travel with your team—or for how long—it's essential to behave respectfully at all times. This reflects common courtesy as well as good sportsmanship.

When traveling with your team, be sure to follow all the rules put in place by your coaches, chaperones, drivers, and anyone else in charge. These rules are in place to ensure everyone's safety and well-being. Be sure to use proper manners and treat everyone respectfully, from fellow teammates to opponents. It's your responsibility to set a good example as a representative of your team and athletic organization. In addition, keep in mind that you are a guest away from home. It's important to demonstrate your gratitude at each stage of your travel journey by being polite and friendly.

Team travels also require patience and understanding on everyone's part, especially if changes, delays, or other inconveniences come up. Be as supportive and agreeable as possible, listen carefully to directions, and stay calm. Adhering to travel etiquette will make the travel experience more pleasant for everyone and help you create good memories with your team.

[94]
ADVICE

It can feel intimidating at times to ask for help because it involves being vulnerable. Most people don't like revealing that they don't understand something or aren't sure what to do. This is especially true for new athletes who are still learning about their sport and how to play but feel reluctant to express their need for guidance.

There are some good strategies for seeking advice from others, such as asking specific questions and being direct. For example, asking your coach how to be a good tennis player is too general. Instead, it's better to identify what type of guidance you need and phrase it in a polite yet assertive manner: "Coach, I'm not sure that my serve is as accurate as it should be. Can you give me some advice to improve my accuracy?"

You should also ask for clarification if you don't understand the directions you're given. Everyone learns differently, and specific phrasing may make sense to one person but be confusing for another. This is especially true when describing movement, so don't hesitate to ask for more information or further explanation of a certain move, strategy, or technique.

Timing is important when asking for advice as well. Be sure that you remain considerate when asking for help, as many people have busy schedules. Be patient and allow the person time to think and respond.

The more you practice politely asking for advice or expressing that you need help, the easier it will be. Most coaches and mentors are happy to answer questions and provide support when they can. Seeking knowledge and clarification is a valuable life skill that can help you avoid misunderstandings and confusion, as well as give you useful strategies for communication. In addition, you'll develop the confidence to admit that you need further information or guidance, which will benefit you in the long run.

[95]
MULTI-SPORT
ATHLETES

Most athletes give different sports a try even at the professional level. As a young athlete, exploring multiple sports is an excellent opportunity to discover your hidden athletic skills. You may find that you have natural talent in a sport that you hadn't previously considered, which can bring you enjoyment as a player and open up new paths to athletic success.

Exploring multiple sports is also an excellent method of cross-training, avoiding burnout, and making new personal connections. Different sports require different movements and techniques, which can build your strength, agility, and endurance in new ways. This gives your body with a break from the repetitive movement of one sport and allows your mind to focus on developing new skills.

Since regularly playing a sport requires a commitment of time and effort, it may seem challenging to explore other options. However, you can approach trying different sports informally through occasional pick-up games or short sessions at your local recreation center. This allows you to participate without undermining any dedication to your primary sport, especially in the off-season. For example, you may decide to take up a few weeks of swimming in the summer while on break from playing hockey in the winter.

In the end, no matter what you try, it's great to keep an open mind when it comes to different sports. You might be surprised what you learn about yourself in the process!

[96]
YOUR PERSONAL BRAND

When most people think of an athlete's personal brand, they probably call to mind professional athletes and their sponsors or partnerships with certain companies. Many athletes lend their names and images to various products, from athletic gear to sneakers, cereals to car insurance.

Since it's unlikely that you'll receive any corporate endorsements, it may seem unusual to consider your "personal brand" as a nonprofessional. However, it's important to understand the impression you make as a player even at a young age.

Your personal brand isn't built from the products or equipment you use but rather the image you create of yourself within your sport. In other words, you make an impact on your fellow players, coaches, officials, and fans by how you carry and present yourself as a person. If you show respect, demonstrate good sportsmanship, and support your teammates, you'll create a positive impression in the sports world. This image reflects your personal brand of being a hardworking, responsible, and courteous player, all of which will encourage others to enjoy being around you.

Unfortunately, there are some young athletes who give a negative impression when playing their sport. This can be due to problematic behaviors such as being inconsiderate, demonstrating unsportsmanlike conduct, or acting with arrogance on and off the field. Building this type of troublesome personal brand is counterproductive; people may start to avoid playing and associating with you. Overall, it's essential to understand that the way people see you reflects your inner character, so you should strive to make a positive impact in your sports world.

[97]
POSTURE
AWARENESS

When you think of posture, the phrase "stand up straight" may come to mind. Most people don't give a lot of thought to their posture, but it's an important part of your overall health and well-being. Essentially, your posture is the way you hold your body when you're standing or sitting. A habit of bad posture can negatively affect your performance and increase the likelihood of injury.

Poor posture can result in rounded shoulders, back pain, muscle fatigue, circulation problems, and headaches. Young athletes are more at risk now than ever due to lack of movement throughout the day. For example, extended time spent sitting while scrolling on phones, playing video games, or even doing homework on the computer can contribute to poor posture. This can negatively affect your endurance, breathing, and joints, which increases the risk of injury and decreases athletic performance.

If you're unsure about the quality of your posture, consult your trainer or doctor. They can help you make adjustments if needed and teach you to position your body in optimal ways. Remember that maintaining good posture will allow you to move more quickly, efficiently, and fluidly. It also improves your balance and protects your body from musculoskeletal injuries. It's important to be aware of how you're standing and sitting, limit your screen time, and be sure to move your body often during the day so that you get plenty of exercise.

[98]
RECOVERY DAYS

You should schedule at least one day a week to rest and recover from the demands of your sport. Not only does this provide a much-needed break for your body and mind, but it also allows time for fun and other tasks you need to complete. Just as weekends are important for getting a break from school, recovery days from athletics are essential for a balanced lifestyle.

Of course, scheduling rest days for yourself is more beneficial and worthwhile when you use that time in a positive manner. Some young athletes may be tempted to practice, do a workout, or even strategize about their sport during recovery days. Unfortunately, this is counterproductive to the purpose of having time off to focus on your well-being, responsibilities, and other hobbies.

It's much healthier to take a complete break from practicing or even *thinking* about your sport. This will give your mind and body complete rest and help you avoid burnout. In addition, you'll feel refreshed and energized when you return to practices, training, and competitive events.

There are many things you can do on your rest days to boost your physical and mental well-being while taking a break from your sport. Spending time with family and friends, catching up on studying or homework, or reading a book are all healthy ways to allow your mind and body to recover from athletics and the pressures it can bring.

As always, it's important to drink plenty of water, eat nutritious food, and practice mindful relaxation on recovery days. This includes getting enough quality sleep. Resting will improve your performance when you get back on the field and establish good habits for self-care throughout your life.

[99]
STAYING
GROUNDED

No matter where your athletic journey takes you, it's important to remember and appreciate your roots, acknowledging the beginnings of your sports path and the people who supported you each step of the way. All journeys include successes and achievements, but they also involve obstacles and setbacks. Therefore, it's essential reflect on where you started, what you've overcome and accomplished, and all the reasons to feel grateful and humble for your experience.

Sometimes, the more successful we become in a certain area of life — such as athletics — the more difficult it is to stay grounded. In this case, being grounded means having a sense of who you are, your values, and how to be humble. Of course, you deserve to be proud of your progress and achievements; however, it's important to avoid growing arrogant or developing an overconfident attitude, which can imply that you lack gratitude and demonstrate poor sportsmanship.

Some strategies that can help you stay grounded are to treat people with respect, both inside and outside your sports world, and recognize the accomplishments of others. Giving back to your community and expressing thanks to the people in your life are also positive ways to remember your roots and appreciate your journey.

Remember that all athletes start at the beginning and make mistakes along the way. Staying grounded will help you maintain a realistic viewpoint, grateful outlook, and modest nature.

[100]
GROWTH
MINDSET

If you think back to where you began as a young athlete, you'll probably be amazed at all you've learned and accomplished. Whether you're playing a few seasons just for fun or it eventually becomes a lifelong activity, sports allow you to grow and improve in many ways. This creates a growth mindset for the future as you apply your newfound self-confidence to other areas of your life, including academics, career paths, hobbies, and even relationships.

If you experience moments when you felt unmotivated, uninspired, or unsure of yourself, look back at how much you've accomplished as an athlete. Just deciding to commit to something new — and believing in yourself enough to try — demonstrates your potential for growth and strength.

The more you believe in yourself and develop self-confidence in your abilities, the more opportunities you'll have to grow and achieve. This may include playing at a higher level such as an all-star team or even participating in other sports and activities. It's important to understand that this process takes patience, time, and experience. It also involves personal reflection and considering how far you've come along your sports journey. In the meantime, you can be proud of what you've learned as a young athlete and continue to set and reach your goals over time — not just in sports but in all aspects of your life.

[101]
TEACHING

As you gain expertise in playing your sport and develop higher-level skills, consider sharing your experience and knowledge with younger athletes. This is a way to share your athletic passion while inspiring and motivating others who've decided to start their own sports journeys.

There are many ways to pass on your knowledge and experience to younger athletes. If you have siblings, cousins, or younger neighbors who are interested in your sport, offer to give them guidance and even help them practice. You can also reach out to your coaches or a sports organization to discover opportunities to volunteer at community events or athletic clinics for younger players. If you have a creative side, you might also consider starting a blog to write about positive experiences from your sports journey for others to read, learn from, and enjoy.

Passing on your knowledge and expertise not only benefits others, but it also gives you an opportunity to reflect on how far you've come in your own athletic journey. This includes all the victories and meaningful memories you've experienced as well as any obstacles and losses that you were able to overcome.

Inspiring younger athletes is also a way to show gratitude and acknowledge the people who influenced and motivated you throughout your athletic experience. This allows you to take pride in the commitment, effort, resilience, and growth you have shown in playing sports and pay that forward to others who are just starting out.

CONCLUSION

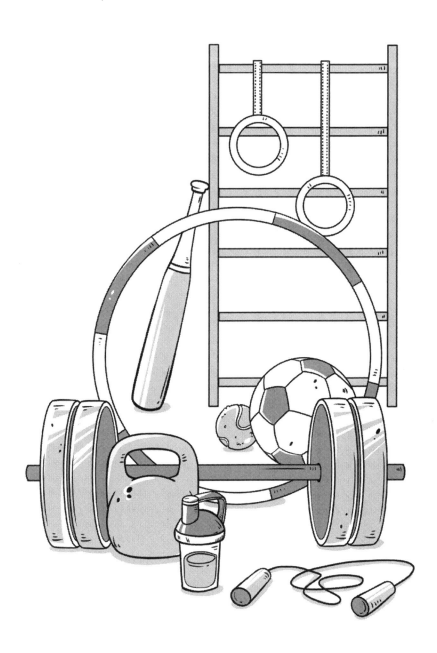

No matter where you are on your athletic journey or how far you expect to go, it's important to realize that playing a sport is an investment in yourself for both the present and the future. Being an athlete at any level and in any sport is a unique opportunity to learn about your personal potential for growth and create memories that will last a lifetime. In addition, participating in sports offers young athletes the chance to meet and befriend diverse groups of people, benefit from physical activity, and learn the value of teamwork and commitment.

Deciding to play a sport and finding the one that works best for you can be challenging. There are many things to consider, including the time commitment, how it will affect your academics and other activities, and your overall goals. The strategies and information in this guide can help you make those decisions by illustrating important things you should know as a young athlete.

If you've already chosen a sport, this book will help you balance athletics with other activities and commitments in your life and show you how to prioritize your health and well-being to avoid burnout. You can apply this knowledge to all areas of your life, including education, relationships, careers, and other pursuits in your future.

A large part of participating in sports is learning how to be a positive and valuable member of a team. That's why we've reinforced principles such as sportsmanship, gratitude, respect, appreciation of diversity, and leadership. Whether your competitions are based on individual or team performance, young athletes must understand how to work with others and regulate their responses to victories and defeats.

Overcoming personal challenges and supporting others for the good of a sport, team, or organization is not only helpful in developing resilience and perseverance but also in navigating future relationships and group dynamics. Research shows that young athletes are likely to demonstrate increased social responsibility and empathy for others in addition to achieving educational and career successes in the future.

Although it may seem like 101 is an awful lot of things to know as a young athlete, your sports journey and experiences will be unique, and you are likely to learn even more! It's important to remember that your athletic path will include physical, emotional, and mental challenges, but these will be balanced with growth, achievements, and fun memories.

In addition to *101 Things Every Young Athlete Should Know*, you should find other sources of support, such as your coaches, trainers, fellow athletes, and parents or guardians. These people can offer advice, serve as mentors, and offer a sense of community when you need help or guidance.

If you take full advantage of your experience as a young athlete, you'll also learn the lifelong importance of caring for your body and your mind. Above all, your sports journey should be about pursuing your goals, connecting with others, and becoming your best self—no matter what sport you play or for how long. Always do your best, take care of yourself, and enjoy the fun and excitement of the sports world!

Made in the USA
Columbia, SC
17 December 2024

49624041R00076